CITY *of* REFUGE

CITY *of* REFUGE

A Novel by

Ashley King

Alachua, Florida 32615

Bridge-Logos
Alachua, FL 32615 USA

City of Refuge
by Ashley King

Edited by Hollee J. Chadwick

Printed in the United States of America.

Library of Congress Catalog Card Number: 2010920251
International Standard Book Number 978-0-88270-481-4

Unless otherwise indicated, Scripture quotations in this book are from the *King James Version* of the Bible.

G218.316.N.m1001.35240

Dedication

To Daddy,
who asked me to help him roof a house one day.

Part One

In the beginning . . .

1

Wynn

"Read me a story, please?" the five-year-old begged for the sixth time.

Wynn held up her hands covered in clay and slip. "I can't, Hope. I have to finish this."

"You misspelled psychology," a dark-haired boy said from the desk crammed in the corner of the room. He flipped a page and took a huge bite of his fourth hotdog. Ketchup spurted from the bun and onto the crisp white pages of the paper he was proofreading.

"Gabe!"

Gabriel tried to clean the ketchup off with his fingers, smearing the page with red.

"Sorry. You misspelled psychology. You were going to have to reprint it anyway."

Wynn sighed.

"When you're finished will you read to me?" Hope asked again, climbing onto the dining chair beside her. She held up a well-worn copy of *Horton Hears a Who*.

"Yes, Hope, when I'm finished I'll read to you, but not

now. Ask Caleb to."

"Pick a card, any card. Come on, Wynn. I've been practicing this one," Caleb requested, entering the cramped dining room from the living room.

"Caleb, I don't have time to pick a card. I have to get this finished."

"What is it?" he demanded, hovering over her sculpture. The bed sheet he had tied around his neck brushed against her butter tub of slip. The container wobbled. Wynn reached for it with both hands at the same time that Caleb did. Fifty-two cards and her clay bust went airborne. Wynn lunged for her sculpture. The liquefied slip splashed all over the table. The clay head hit the floor and the cards floated down around it. Wynn stared in horror at the broken remains of her art project. The chin lay across the room, the nose had crumbled, and half the skull had been bashed in.

Caleb looked with wide eyes at the deformed lump of clay. Gabriel left the desk to come view the scene. He shoved his last bite of hotdog in his mouth.

"You killed George Washington. That's not very patriotic."

"What happened? Oh." Wynn's other sister neared. She looked at Caleb. "Did you do this?"

Slowly, he nodded, his eyes still round with fear.

Chassity looked from the clay to her sister's face. She nodded. "You better run."

Taking her advice, Caleb fled the room, his yellow bed sheet cape fluttering behind him. Wynn wasted no time. She took off after her brother at top speed.

"Caleb!" she screeched, flying after him. He dodged her miry hands and darted through the living room.

"What's going on?" demanded their father from the

recliner. Their mother jumped out of her speeding children's path.

"Wynn, your hands!"

"Run, Caleb, run!" Gabriel cheered, appearing in the room to watch the spectacle. Caleb circled the recliner, stumbling over his father's outstretched feet.

"She's going to kill me!" Caleb shrieked. He jumped over the coffee table and ran down the hallway. Wynn followed suit, tripped over the wooden table, and landed face first on the stained carpet. The slamming door shook the small house as Caleb made his escape into the room he shared with his brother.

Wynn took a long moment to lift her head. When she did she found the majority of her family staring at her. Her father leaned over, resting his forearms on his thighs, and quirked an eyebrow.

"You okay?"

Wynn's lip quivered. She looked at her twin brother who had ruined her science report, Chassity who was thoroughly enjoying her big sister's predicament, and Hope who had been annoying her all evening. She glanced toward the dining room where her bust of George Washington lay smashed on the floor. Week's worth of work. And now her nose hurt. Tears welled up in her eyes.

"Oh, Wynn! Your nose is bleeding!" her mother exclaimed, reaching for the box of tissue on the TV stand. Wynn wiped her nose and burst into uncontrollable laughter, the tears spilling forth.

"Caleb!" Wynn yelled, holding a tissue to her nose, giggling and crying all at once. "I'm so mad," *hiccup*, "at you!"

"I'm sorry, Wynn. I didn't mean to kill him!" Caleb

wailed from behind the locked bedroom door. Confused, her father looked to her mother.

"We have very odd kids."

"What happened?" Her mother held out another tissue.

Chassity brought forth the remains of Wynn's A+ project. Hope held up her "Horton" book. Gabriel produced the crimson-stained report.

"We did."

2

Alex

Alex rolled over, burying his head deeper in the pillow. What was that noise? He cracked an eye and tried to focus his blurry, morning vision on his alarm clock. The room was still dark. Gray light seeped in through the window and rain hammered against the glass.

His bedroom door slammed open. The door handle bumped against the drywall, gouging a hole in the wall. A tall, slender woman wearing a terrycloth robe and large curlers in her hair came striding into the room. A purple toothbrush dangled from her mouth. She lugged in a wicker basket filled with folded laundry.

"Get your lazy rear out of bed. I've been pounding on your door for the past five minutes. You're late." The toothbrush bobbed up and down as she spoke. She dropped the basket onto the only clean space on the floor.

"What? Why didn't my alarm go off?" Alex demanded, reaching for his clock.

"It's been storming all night. The electricity went out. Come on. Up, up, up!" his mother replied, scrubbing her molars between words. Alex swung his legs over the side of the bed, using his favorite swear word as he did so.

"Watch your mouth, young man," his mother advised through blue toothpaste foam. She gave him a warning glance before leaving his room. Alex made a face at her back before standing up and tripping over the blankets wrapped around his ankles. He fought furiously with the bed linens.

Finally, with a few hard yanks, he freed himself.

He waded through the piles of dirty clothes and other junk that grew on his floor. He stumbled over his guitar and stubbed his toe on a table leg before he finally made it to the basket his mother had just delivered.

"Great. Practice is going to be h—"

"ALEX!"

"I'm coming! Give me a minute, would ya?" he yelled to his mother. He dug through the basket and fished out a pair of jeans and a T-shirt. He didn't have time to gel his hair, so he snatched a well-worn baseball cap from his dresser. His Nikes were under a pile of crumpled song lyrics.

"Mom, I can't find any clean socks," he hollered, not bothering to check his drawers. A rolled up pair flew through his opened door. He caught them and pulled them on. *Mothers were good for something.* He checked the mirror before sauntering toward the kitchen.

"I made toast. Drink a glass of juice. If you leave in five minutes you'll make it to school on time," his mother said as she darted around the room, throwing objects into her briefcase. She padded across the slate floor in blue, satin house slippers. She had forgotten to change her shoes. Alex snared a charred piece of toast from the plate and spread pumpkin butter on the top.

"I'll be late tonight. Order in a pizza when you get home. Your father's flight is supposed to get in at eight. Where on Earth are my keys? You can have some of the boys over, but don't make a mess. Good luck at practice. Here they are. Bye, Alex," she waved at him, her keys dangling from her thumb.

"Mom?"

She stopped mid-stride and turned to face him. "Yeah?"

Alex dipped his chin and looked pointedly at her feet. She glanced down. Groaning in frustration, she tossed her briefcase and purse onto the counter, and dashed toward her bedroom. Alex grinned.

"You need to lay off those caffeine pills, Mom," he commented, before shoving the rest of his toast in his mouth. His mother reappeared, pulling on a navy pump.

"They are not caffeine pills. They increase your metabolic rate so that you burn calories more quickly. Now get to school," she corrected as she retrieved her things and started once more toward the door. She stopped and looked down at her burdened hands.

"Where are my keys?"

Alex pulled his cap onto his head and pushed away from the counter. Snatching up her key ring, he tossed it at her. She nearly dropped everything else trying to catch it.

"See ya later, Mom." He snagged his book bag from the den and his letter jacket from the hall tree.

"Drive safely, Alex. It's really pouring out there. Wrecks are inevitable on days like this. Your Uncle Rob had his wreck on a rainy day just like this. They had to cut him out of the car and his leg was severed. It was horrible," his mother called, balancing everything on one arm while she struggled into her trench coat. Alex rolled his eyes. His uncle had had a six-pack before that car crash.

"Alex?" she called when he didn't reply.

"I'll be careful, Mom. I'll make it to school alive and maybe even with all my limbs," he promised, swinging open the door to the four-car garage.

"I'm serious, Alexander. Drive slowly." He did not reply to his mother's final admonition. She worried too much. His pickup was parked on the far side of the garage next to the wall where his father's unused power tools hung. He threw his bag in and hopped into the cab as his mother struggled with full hands to shut the door. The garage door whirred open as he revved the engine. He glanced at the clock. Putting the truck into reverse, he pulled out onto the asphalt. The rain blurred the world like a cataract and the thunder drowned out his music. He flicked on the headlights and turned the lever for his windshield wipers. Homeroom started in fifteen minutes. He put his foot on the gas pedal. He could make it in ten.

3

Wynn

Wynn pulled a gray hoodie on over her T-shirt.

"You're going to be late. The bus'll be here in ten minutes," Chassity reminded from the mirror. She pulled her red curls back into a ponytail. "I wish my hair was your color."

Wynn stepped up behind her, snatching the brush from her hand. With a few quick movements, her long, reddish brown hair was twisted up and bound with an elastic band. She smoothed the top and fluffed the messy bun she'd made.

"Mom has red hair," she reminded, handing back the brush and going in search of her tennis shoes. Chassity sighed.

"Yeah, but Mom's already married."

Wynn paused trying to understand her sister's statement. "What?"

Chassity plopped down on the edge of Wynn's daybed.

"No one will ever want to date me. Guys don't like red hair," she bemoaned. Wynn poked her arm under her sisters' bunk bed, feeling around for her shoes.

"Chass, you're twelve. Boy's your age could care less if your hair were purple," said the wise and ever so much older Wynn. "Besides you can't date till you're sixteen anyway.

"Have you seen my shoes? Oh gross!" she squealed when her hand encountered something squishy. She pulled out a slimy, half-eaten banana.

"Oh, my banana! I lost that when I was getting ready

for bed last night," Chassity explained, rubbing at the freckles on her nose. "I hate freckles. I wish my skin were like yours."

Wynn dropped the rotting bedtime snack in the wastebasket and wiped her hand on a tissue. She pulled open the closet door.

"I have freckles, too. Where are my shoes?"

"But you have cute freckles, just on your nose. Everyone always talks about how cute your freckles are," Chassity whined. Wynn rolled her eyes.

"Chassity, I need my shoes. Can I sympathize with you over your freckles at a more convenient moment?"

"They're in the dining room. Remember you took them off after you came in from choir practice, when you started working on your art project," Chassity supplied with a generous air. She sighed. "I should have picked them up for you. I was going to, but then Caleb knocked over your project and I cleaned up that mess. Remember?"

Wynn shook her head a little. Her younger sister liked to think of herself as the family martyr. "Yes, and thank you."

She grabbed her bag and hurried from the room.

"Here, Wynn. I put it in a plastic folder." Gabriel shoved her science report in her hands as soon as she entered the living room. He nodded and bit his Pop Tart in half. Wynn flipped open the folder, scanning the text she had retyped.

"It's okay then, you think."

"Definitely an A minus," he assured confidently. Wynn nodded and shoved the folder into her backpack.

"It's nice having a science geek for a twin brother," she said with an affectionate grin. "Even if he does spill ketchup on my first draft."

"I'll take that as a compliment."

"Mornin', Sweetheart," her dad greeted, draping a tie around his neck as he entered the room. "Mornin', Gabe."

"Morning, Daddy."

"Morning, Dad."

"Wynn, Gabe. Come eat breakfast. Your bus will be here soon," their mother called from the kitchen. Wynn dropped her bag by the front door and headed for the joined dining room and kitchen.

"I made you a bowl of Lucky Charms, Wynn," a puppy-dog-eyed Caleb announced when he spotted her. He held up a plastic bowl of soggy cereal and bleeding marshmallows.

"He's been waiting for you with that cereal for an hour," their mother explained. She kissed her husband, before setting to work on his tie. "Good morning, Mr. Redecke."

"Morning, Beautiful."

Caleb set the bowl down and ran over to where Wynn had placed the remains of her clay sculpture on the desk.

"I put his nose back on. See?"

Wynn observed the extra credit project she had been working on for two weeks. The work that had once resembled the majestic first president now looked like a Sesame Street character.

"Caleb. That was his chin."

Caleb looked crestfallen. Gabriel burst into a deep laugh that squeaked upon completion. Hope, eating apple cinnamon oatmeal, rubbed her nose on the ruffled sleeve of her flannel nightgown.

"I told you that wasn't his nose, Caleb." She patted her oatmeal smooth with her spoon. "His nose wasn't that big before. That's how I knew."

Their father came close and studied the piece. "You

could say it's modern art. Modern art doesn't have to look like anything," he suggested, poking at the new, bulbous nose.

"You could just explain what happened. I'm sure Mrs. Osman will understand," Wynn's mother said, handing her daughter a package of Pop Tarts.

"I'm sorry, Wynn. I didn't mean to. I really didn't," ten-year-old Caleb interjected, his blue eyes filling with tears. Wynn shrugged. She had been furious at her brother the night before, but the project had been for extra credit and its destruction would not hurt her grade.

"I know, Caleb. I'm not mad at you anymore."

The brother threw his arms around her, glad to be forgiven for his terrible crime.

"Wynn, Gabe! The bus is here!" Chassity announced from the living room.

"Kisses," their mother reminded when they started to dart off. Dutifully, Gabriel returned to peck his mother on the cheek. Hope raised her arms to him and puckered her sticky lips. He bent and accepted the oatmeal smothered kiss. His father nodded over his coffee cup.

"See ya tonight, Sport."

Wynn made her rounds. "Bye, Momma," she punctuated with a kiss on the cheek.

"Bye, Daddy." He kissed the top of her head.

"Bye."

"Bye, Hope," she said, receiving a sloppy kiss and tight squeeze. Caleb gave her a hug and a last apology.

"I'm sorry, Wynn. I won't ever make you pick a card again," he solemnly promised.

"Wynn, Gabe!" Chassity prompted.

Wynn squeezed her little brother tight. She couldn't

stay mad at him.

"Bye, Caleb. See y'all tonight."

Her family chorused one last goodbye to her and her brother. The two of them sprinted through the living room, snatching book bags and jackets.

"Take your umbrellas. It's pouring outside," their mother called after them. Chassity stood at the door, dutifully holding two faded, torn umbrellas.

"Bye, Chass," Gabe farewelled, running out into the rain without the umbrella. Wynn accepted her sister's offering.

"Don't run or your jeans will get soaked," Chassity warned. Wynn nodded and rolled her eyes.

"No running. Got it. Have fun at school, Chass." With a smile at her fifty-year wise, twelve-year-old sister, she stepped out the door into a drenching rain.

4

Alex

Alex popped a stick of Juicy Fruit in his mouth and sucked on it for a moment before biting into it. He had left his high-class neighborhood a few miles back and now he was on a narrow, twisting road that would shorten his trip by half. The road cut through fields and then snaked down a steep wooded incline that the kids at school called the Devil's Backbone. When he was sixteen, he and the rest of the football team had raced motorcycles down it. His best friend, Taylor, had lost control and went over the side. He and his motorcycle had tumbled down the ravine and finally banged against a tree. Taylor had broken both legs and an arm and spent a year in physical therapy. Now they joked about doing it again sometime, but they all knew they were just bluffing. The stupidity had been scared out of them when Taylor went over the edge.

Up ahead of him a small car pulled out of a gravel driveway and began puttering along.

"Oh, come on! Could you go any slower?" he demanded of the driver. The rain had slacked off slightly making it much easier to see. Alex's cell phone began to vibrate in his coat pocket. He hit the power button on his radio and pulled the phone out.

"Chadwell."

"Alex, it's Mom," the caller announced. He rolled his eyes, and tapped on the steering wheel. The driver in front of him was poking along at forty miles an hour.

"Yup?"

"Hey, I'm on Route 4, and the road is flooded over. I want you to call me as soon as you get to school."

"Mom, I'll be fine. I've driven in the rain before." His windshield was beginning to steam up. He hit the defrost button.

"I know you have. Just do what I told you and call me, okay?"

"Yeah. Mom. I gotta go. Bye."

He tossed the phone onto the seat beside his bag. His mother must suffer from chronic paranoia. She annoyed the living daylights out of him. He pounded the button on his radio again and N'Sync filled the cab. *Ugh!* He changed the station.

The sooty black sky was split by a blinding flash. The crack of thunder was deafening. A large branch fell to the road just ahead. The small car's brake lights glowed red. It swerved to the right, moving dangerously close to the edge. Alex pounded his brakes to the floorboard. His truck began to hydroplane. The car slowed and bumped into the thick limb. Alex spun the wheel to the left, hoping to miss the car and hit the branch on the left side. The bed of his truck began to fishtail. A sickening crunch filled his ears as the tail of the truck collided with the car. Alex felt as if his entire world were spinning. Everything was happening in slow motion. His forehead hit the steering wheel. He saw black.

5

Alex

Alex raised his head and stared at the dashboard. The music was blaring. His foot was pressing the brake pedal to the floor. He was breathing heavily and his hands gripped the steering wheel. He looked around. He couldn't see through the smoke. The stench of burned rubber filled his nostrils. He sat dazed for a long moment willing his heart rate to slow. Finally, he pushed the gearshift into park. Slowly, he eased himself out of his truck. The rain pounded on his jacket and sounded tinny as it hit the hot metal of his smashed pickup. The small car that had been on the road ahead of him was gone.

"Oh, God, no, please no." His legs were heavy as he ran to the edge of the asphalt. He held his breath as he peered over the edge. Saplings and underbrush were uprooted. The wet earth was scraped smooth. Steam wafted up from the twisted metal smashed against a stand of ash trees twenty feet down the tor. Alex felt sick. He fell to his knees on the graveled shoulder. For a long moment, he knelt there, stunned, staring at the wreckage.

Pushing himself up, he ran back to his truck, wrenching the door open. He fumbled on the seat for his cell phone. He finally spotted it on the passenger floorboard. His fingers trembled as he dialed.

"911. What's your emergency?" the operator's voice sounded thick, as if it were coming from behind glass.

"There's been a car wreck. We hit. Oh, God, help me!"

"Sir, please try to calm down. Can you give me your location?" the voice questioned. It took long moments for her words to register. He started moving toward the ravine.

"Sir?"

"The Devil's Backbone."

"Is that Old Piper Mill Road?"

He paused. He heard something. He turned his head, straining to hear.

"Sir?"

"Piper. Yeah, Piper. Someone's crying!" The sound was low and muffled.

"Sir, are there any injuries?"

"Someone's crying! Oh, dear Lord! There was a kid!"

"Sir? Sir?"

Alex dropped the phone on the ground. He had never prayed before, but he did now.

"Oh, God, please, please," he said over and over again through chattering teeth. He reached for a slender Maple and dug his heel into the soft mud. He reached for the next nearest tree, branches, anything firm. Slowly he slipped and slid down the incline. The crying was growing quieter.

"Hold on!" he shouted. "Hold on! I'm coming." His foot slipped. He fell hard, slamming against a tree trunk. He heard something crack and pain surged through his leg.

"Hold on," he whispered. Using the tree, Alex pulled himself to his feet. The sudden burst of pain in his leg made his breath catch and his head pound. He was nearly to the car now. The muffler had been knocked loose. The machine was growling. The raindrops sizzled as they landed on the exposed engine. The car was bent around two thick tree trunks. Glass was everywhere. Reaching the back door, Alex fell against the car with a thud. The crying had stopped.

Pushing himself up, he stared into the car.

Red. Everything is red.

A woman was slumped over the twisted steering wheel. Her long hair covered her face and was black with blood. The door and the dashboard against her crushed body. In the passenger seat, a smaller form was entrapped by gnarled metal. In the back seat was a boy, slouched on his side, his face buried against the back of the seat in front of him. Just inside the window was a small girl, strapped tightly in a booster seat. Her little legs were crushed by the seat, pierced by the exposed coils. The door was crunched in around her and the glass had sliced her round face. She was still wearing her nightgown. Against her cheek was cushioned a stuffed animal soaked through with crimson-tinged rain.

"Who are you?" she whispered. Tears poured down Alex's cheeks, dropping and mingling with the rain and blood on her face.

"Everything's gonna be alright. You just hold on, okay?" he choked. His voice was raspy.

The little girl's eyes were intensely green.

"Are you an angel?" she asked. Her young voice gurgled and she coughed. "I'm scared, Angel. Hold my hand?"

A cry escaped Alex's throat. "You hang on. Just hold onto me."

He reached through the broken window, wrapping his numb fingers around her tiny hand. It was so cold.

Sirens screamed faintly in the distance. Lights, red and blue, flashed. He heard shouts. The rain tinkled on the broken windshield. He could hear her heavy breathing. Then he couldn't.

The paramedics dragged him away.

6

Wynn

"How bad is it? Could we fix it if I came over tonight and helped?" the slender blonde asked, shoving her pink bag into her overflowing locker. Wynn slid her Algebra book off the shelf.

"Ashleigh, I don't think there's any hope for him. He looks like this." Wynn demonstrated, contorting her features as hideously as she could. The third freshman girl standing near smoothed on tinted lip-gloss and smacked her lips. She puckered in front of her locker mirror and tucked a strand of light hair back.

"I would have killed my brother if he did that to my project."

"Becky, you're an only child," Ashleigh reminded.

"If I had a brother and if he ruined my homework, I would kill him," Rebecca expounded in annoyance.

"Then you would be an only child again," Ashleigh pointed out.

Rebecca rolled her eyes. "Anyway, enough about annoying—" she shot a look to Ashleigh, "—siblings. Let's run by the vending machines. I'm about to die of thirst."

"You're such a drama queen," Wynn said with a laugh.

"And proud of it. Can I borrow a quarter?" she requested, pulling some change, a crumpled tissue, and lint from her pocket. "Hey what's your dad doing here?"

Wynn looked down the hall. Ashleigh's father was exiting the offices. He walked slowly, his face solemn.

Ashleigh shrugged. "He's probably here to have lunch with Mom."

"At nine-thirty in the morning?" Rebecca demanded sarcastically. "Sometimes you're not the brightest crayon, Ashleigh Osman."

Ashleigh's hands flew to her hips.

"Remind me again why we're friends."

Wynn stepped between the two. "Because you've known one another since preschool and you both have sweet hearts," she glanced at Rebecca, "somewhere."

Ashleigh snickered and Rebecca stuck out her tongue.

"Wynn?"

The three girls turned around to face Ashleigh's father. He looked uncomfortable and tugged on his suit coat.

"Wynn, I'd like to speak to you," he announced. The three students shared a look of confusion.

"Uh, sure Mr. Osman. I'll catch up with you two in a minute," she told her friends. She noticed the glance the detective gave his daughter.

"Actually Ashleigh, I'd like for you to wait with the assistant principal," he told her. Thoroughly confused, the two girls followed him to the office. Dr. Becker, the principal, was waiting in her doorway.

"Hello, Wynn. Please, come in and have a seat. Gabriel. You come in, too."

Wynn turned to see her brother being escorted into the lobby by the assistant principal.

"Wynn? Detective Osman? What's going on?" Gabe demanded, his brow furrowed in suspicion.

"Please, have a seat in Dr. Becker's office and we'll tell you exactly what's happened."

Wynn stepped into her office with her brother's hand at

her back. She dropped into a plush upholstered chair and set her books on her lap. The adults shut the door and then turned to face them. Detective Osman looked tortured and the principal looked pitiful.

There was a sinking feeling in her stomach. She felt suddenly hollow and fear echoed inside her. Gabe sat down beside her and she reached for his hand.

"Your mother took your younger brother and sister to school today," the detective began.

"She does everyday. They go to the elementary school, but they don't like riding the bus 'cuz their bus ride is an hour long. She can get them there in ten minutes," Gabe explained. "Dad always leaves at the same time for church."

Detective Osman nodded and clenched his jaw. He turned his back to them for a moment, before facing them again. He squatted in front of them.

"This morning there was an accident."

"Daddy? Is he all right?" Wynn demanded, leaning forward and squeezing Gabe's hand tighter. The man shook his head.

"It's not your father. It's your mother and your brother and your sisters." The tears pooled in his eyes. "Wynn, Gabe I am so sorry. They didn't make it."

Wynn shook her head. "No."

"Wynn, it happened about an hour ago. Your father wanted to come for you. He was too upset. We escorted him home. He's waiting for you. Your grandparents are there."

"No," she calmly said again. She released her brother's hand. Gabe sat staring—his face a portrait of shock.

"We're going to take you home now."

Wynn stood up from her seat. Her books dropped to

the floor and the chair toppled backward.

"No!" she repeated with more force. "No. They're fine. My mother's at home. She's washing laundry. Hope's at the kitchen table coloring. Chassity, Caleb, they're at school. You're confused. They're fine. They'll be at home when the bus drops us off.

"Now, I'm late for Algebra. I'm sorry, I have to go." She turned and reached for the doorknob. Detective Osman reached out and put his hands on her shoulders. Wynn felt the room begin to spin. *They were fine. They were all fine. They had to be fine.* She wanted to push the detective away but her arms wouldn't move.

"Gabe?" she called out pitifully. He didn't answer. He just stared. "Gabe! Gabriel, say it. Tell me they're all right. Tell me!" she screamed, but he said nothing. And then she was just screaming. Her body convulsed with sobs. She went down on her knees and Detective Osman lowered her to the ground, holding her as she cried out. And Gabe just stared.

7

Alex

Alex opened his eyes and stared blankly at speckled ceiling tiles. *Where am I?* He struggled to sit up.

"Alex? Honey, lie still. How do you feel?" His mother's face suddenly hovered above his own. Alex was completely confused.

"Horrible. What's going on?" he demanded, lifting a hand to shield the light from his eyes. His head was throbbing in rhythm with his pulse.

"You're in a hospital room. Honey, you were in an accident."

Immediately it all came rushing back. The crushing metal, the squealing tires sounded in his ears. His muscles tensed, readying for impact. *The little girl, how was the little girl?* He sat up and clutched the bedrail.

"The people in the car, the little girl. Are they all right? Mom, please tell me they're all right."

There were tears in his mother's eyes.

"Mom?"

His mother took his hand in both hers. She stared at the blankets.

"They're gone, Alex."

Alex fell back into the hard pillows. The room was growing warm. The bed began spinning.

"I'm going to throw up."

8

Wynn

The moonlight dripped in through the closed blinds and covered the room with dim stripes of light. The numbers on the clock glowed green. It had been hours since Grandma Red had sat on the bed and rocked her as she cried. Now she lay in the bedroom her grandparents had fixed especially for visits from their grandkids. Gabriel was on the second twin bed. His breathing was heavy and she knew he was asleep. He hadn't said a word since that morning.

Wynn felt drained and numb. She kept waiting for Chassity to mumble something in her sleep or for Hope to shake her awake and ask her to take her to the potty. But they couldn't. They weren't there. Wynn wasn't even in the room she shared with them.

She needed a glass of water. She swung her legs over the bed, letting the carpet tickle the bottoms of her feet. She felt her way to the door, tripping over the duffle bags her aunt had packed for them. Her grandparents' house had a nightlight in every room. The hallway had two. She stumbled past the master bedroom and the room where her father slept. The fish tank hummed in the den and cast blue light into the hallway. In the great room, the grandfather clock chimed the quarter hour. The sound was loud and old. Wynn hurried past the doorway. She felt suddenly afraid of the dark and the quiet. She crossed the threshold and into the kitchen, her toes curling involuntarily when her bare feet touched the cold tile. Finding a Mason jar in the cabinet, she filled it full of water. She started toward the kitchen table but jumped when she noticed the slouched figure sitting there.

"Daddy?" she whispered, drawing closer to the table. The man stirred and even in the dim nightlight glow, she could see the tears on his face. His eyes were glassy and his hair mussed.

"Why? Why would God let this happen? Why would He take her away? Why my babies? It's not fair." His voice was thin and raw. Wynn shuddered.

She didn't know why God had taken them. She had never questioned Him before, never doubted Him, never really paid much attention to Him at all. Now she wanted to scream at Him. She wanted to yell out how much she hated Him for this. After all her family had done for Him. Was this the way God repaid people who had given their everything to Him?

Wynn looked to her father. She had never seen him broken before. He had never doubted his God. She wanted to crawl up in his lap and have him rock her like he did when she was young, but he couldn't help her. And she couldn't help him.

"I'm sorry, Daddy," she whispered, then turned and fled the room. By the time she reached the bedroom her throat was raw with swallowed tears and her eyes burned. She set the brimming glass on the nightstand and fell into her bed, stifling her sobs with her pillow. Her family was gone and God had left her.

9

Alex

Alex had retold the story to the police three times. He just wanted to go home. He wanted to get away from all the prying, sympathy, and the watery hospital Jell-O. His mother was at the bedside with her hand on his shoulder. His father sat listening and taking notes at a small table in the corner of the room.

"So the child was alive when you reached her," the officer verified. Alex closed his eyes and laid his head against the pillows.

"Yes."

The police officer tapped the pad with the tip of his pencil. He glanced over his notes, making a correction, and then closed the notebook.

"Well, I guess this is all I need. We'll contact you as soon as the report is finished. Thank you." The middle-aged man stood. He nodded toward Alex's mother and then to his father before leaving the room.

"Are you ready to go home? The doctor has released you," his mother announced as soon as the officer had left. Alex sighed with relief.

"They may take you to court, you know," his father said suddenly from his place at the table. He had been drilling Alex for details. He was already planning his son's defense.

"It was an accident, Darren. It wasn't Alex's fault," his wife said. Darren Chadwell shook his head and held up a copy of the local newspaper. Alex's picture had made the front page just beside a photograph of the Redecke family. The headline read "Local Baptist Church Devastated by Car Crash".

"It doesn't matter, Joan. Those four people are dead. That minister will try to sue us for everything we have. He'd be stupid not to."

"Darren, please, not now. Alex, honey, push the button and we'll have a nurse find us a wheelchair," Joan commanded. Alex did as he was told, anxious to leave. His leg ached in its cast and his broken ribs hurt when he breathed. His entire body, strong after years of football and baseball, felt weak and tired. He wanted to go home, go to sleep, and forget everything.

"We have to face facts, Joan. There is no use sitting around, unprepared for it. This will be a major court battle and the Redecke man will have the sympathy of the public. No juror on earth would not sympathize. The man lost his wife and three of his kids, for heaven's sake."

Joan turned glaring eyes on her husband. "Stop. Just stop. Alex has been through enough for two days."

A nurse's aide entered then, already pushing a wheelchair.

"We were just given the release papers. I'm assuming this is what you were calling for," she said in a cheery voice.

"Yes, thank you," Joan answered with a strained smile. The young woman pushed the chair over, angling it beside the bed, and locked the brakes.

"Would you like help getting into the chair?" she asked. Darren shook his head.

"We'll manage. Thanks." He turned toward Alex. "Well, let's get you home."

Alex nodded in relieved agreement. Home would be wonderful.

10

Wynn

"Ron, the arrangements must be made," Grandma Red told her son at the breakfast table. Ron Redecke kept his eyes on the yellow pine table.

"I can't." He sounded hollow.

Wynn pushed her breakfast around on her plate. How could they be eating grits, biscuits, and gravy as if nothing had happened? Only Gabriel had not come to the table. She reached for the sugar bowl.

Her grandfather put a hand on her father's shoulder.

"Son, I know this is hard. It hurts. It hurts real bad. Times I'll think of 'em and I can't breathe. But this is got to be done. The ceremony and the plots, the . . . the clothes you want 'em wearin', you've got to choose it all. You've got to be strong just now."

Ron pushed back from the table. "I can't do this."

He walked from the room and out the back door, letting it shut quietly behind him.

Wynn stared at her white plate and the ruffled peach placemat. She heard her grandmother sniffle.

"I'll do it. I'll talk to Ivy and we'll handle it. Dear Lord, I never thought I'd see this day."

Papaw Red nodded. "I'll see about the plots and the stones."

Wynn felt the tears stinging her eyes.

"Wynn, darlin', how're you doin'?" Papaw Red asked her. Wynn shrugged her shoulders and wiped her nose on her shirtsleeve. She wasn't doing well at all. Yesterday played over and over in her mind and now here they sat discussing graves and headstones.

"It's all right to cry, Baby," her grandmother told her. There were tears in her eyes as well. "Poor child's lost so much, Lord; we've all lost so much."

"How can you still pray to a God that would take everything away?" Wynn suddenly demanded, her eyes dark with anger. Immediately, her grandmother reached her round arms for her. She pushed Wynn's head onto her shoulder and held it there with her chin.

"Oh, Baby. God didn't want to hurt you. He just couldn't wait to hold 'em any longer."

II

Wynn

Wynn stood with her father and her brother. She did not cry. She had no tears left. People waited in line to hug them or shake their hands and tell them how sorry they were. Wynn wanted to scream at them, to tell them to go away. Their apologies couldn't bring back her family. The way they said they understood how she must feel was a horrible lie.

The minister who was to conduct the funeral took Wynn's father to the side. Immediately her grandmothers came forward to fill the void. Grandma Ivy, her mother's mother, put an arm around her. Her voice was deep and scratchy. She had stopped smoking years ago but the tears had irritated her throat.

"Hon, why don't you and Gabe go and get something to drink. The ceremony'll be starting soon," she suggested around a sniffle. Her eyes were swollen and all her mascara had run. Grandma Red nodded in agreement. Her nose was red and her lips quivered.

"Go on, Baby. Ivy and me'll thank everyone else." She looked to Gabe and gave him a weak smile before swiping at her nose with Papaw Red's handkerchief. Gabriel took his sister by the arm.

"Come on, Wynn," he said quietly, leading her away from the crowd dressed in black.

"I hate this Gabe. I hate having everyone bringing flowers and telling me how sorry they are," Wynn told him as they wandered the funeral home in search of the family's parlor. The deacons' wives had brought two-liters of drinks and sub sandwiches and left them there.

"I know. I do, too. I guess it makes them feel better," Gabe said quietly. He reached for the Dr. Pepper and poured them each a glass. They sat down on the dark, upholstered chairs and stared into their drinks. Wynn could see her shadowed reflection in the fizzing soda.

"I still can't believe it. I keep waiting for Hope to come running over to me. For Momma to come and tell me it's all okay," she hiccupped on a sob. She would forget for a moment and then the truth would dawn on her again. The ache would hit her and take her breath away. She wiped the tears from her eyes.

"So what do we do now? What happens next?" Wynn wondered aloud. She sounded lost and pitiful. Gabriel looked up at the painting of a garden that hung above the buffet that held the sandwiches and plates.

"Gabe?" she prompted, desperately hoping he would talk to her now. He had been so closed up over the past four days. He had hardly spoken and still he had not cried.

"That's what I've been asking myself since it happened. What do I do now that Chassity isn't here to tattle on everything I do? Caleb won't be tagging after me, trying to do everything I do. Hope won't be asking me to play Candyland with her. Mom won't tell me to clean my room or do my homework. All those times I wished they'd go away. I wished they'd all just leave me alone. Well, now I've got it. They've all just left me alone."

12

Alex

"I want to go, Mom. I need to do this."

"Honey, I just don't know. Do you honestly think that going to the cemetery would be good for you? Alex, you've been through so much, I just don't think you need to be there," Joan said softly. She sat in the chair across from where he lay on the leather sofa. She had closed the wooden blinds to darken the room, hoping that he would relax and rest.

"I think the best thing for you to do would be to go on with your normal routine. Go back to school tomorrow, sit on the bench at the next game, go out with your friends."

Alex swallowed hard and stared at the blue fiberglass that covered his leg.

"Mom, I killed four people. I can't go on with my normal routine. How can anything ever be normal again?"

Joan stiffened. "You didn't kill them, Alex. It was all an accident. It was no one's fault. The police are sure to see that."

Alex shook his head. "I was following too closely. If I hadn't tried to swerve around them the impact would have been smaller and straight on, the—"

"There was a limb in the road, the roads were wet—" Joan interrupted but Alex cut her off.

"And they would never have gone over that edge if I hadn't been there."

His mother said nothing. She just stared at the sage walls

as if the answers were written on them. Alex was quiet for a long moment.

"I want to go, Mom. I have to."

13

Wynn

She felt detached, empty. She felt nothing. The navy, velvet canopy shadowed the graves. The minister was speaking. The breeze slipped through the crisp autumn trees. Birds were calling to one another. The sun still shone. How could they be gone when the sun was shining?

She stared at the flowers—the tall white baskets with the braided handles and the urns and the wreathes on their wire stands. They were so ugly. Why would people give such ugly flowers? The hideous, blue, fabric carnations were the worst.

She looked to Gabriel. His face was still a blank mask, devoid of all emotion.

Wynn raised her head. Reverend Christi was praying now. Confusion clouded her mind. Everything she had ever known was changing. Her family was gone. Her father wasn't the same anymore. Gabriel was so quiet, so withdrawn. Her grandparents had grown old in just a few days. They had all been taken from her.

All at once the tears burst forth. Her cries shook the air. She pushed away all the people that reached to comfort her. Reality had come at last. The ones that she loved the most were gone. Life as it had always been was finished. Ended. Dead.

14

Alex

The crowds were dispersing when he topped the hill. The scene was melancholy and beautiful. Figures in black, their faces drawn with sadness, contrasted against the perfect sky and bright, sun-lit trees. The branches were aflame with reds and oranges and golds. Four mounds of earth were buried by flowers of every color.

Alex did not intend to approach the Redeckes. He meant to stay away, watch from a distance, but he found himself drawing nearer.

"Alex," his mother cautioned, placing a cold hand on his arm. He was only fifty feet away now. He could see the family. The father knelt by the graves, his face covered. His dark brown hair was uncombed. His clothes were rumpled. The boy looked like a statue, emotionless, hard. Alex recognized him now. He had just made the junior varsity basketball team. The girl Alex had never noticed before. Now she stood, head down, silent tears bathing her cheeks. He inched closer, drawn to their pain.

She was the first to spot him. She looked up, meeting his eyes, causing his heart to stop. For a moment her face was a reflection of the days she had spent crying. All her pain and sadness was on display, but then recognition registered. Instantly her eyes narrowed. Alex stood paralyzed.

"Alex, I think we had better go," his mother urged at his side. She put her arm around his stooped shoulders and attempted to turn him away, but he did not move.

Gabriel Redecke noticed him. His eyes widened and his jaw dropped. Suddenly, his sister stepped forward.

"What are you doing here?" she demanded. Alex's mother tugged on his arm, silently asking him to just walk away.

"Why have you come?" Gwyneth Redecke asked again. Alex swallowed hard and forced himself to meet the girl's bloodshot eyes. What could he say to her?

Gabriel Redecke approached and put a hand on his sister's shoulder. Their father looked up. His face was wet—his eyes hollow. In a moment, he was standing behind his children.

"You're Alexander Chadwell."

Alex nodded. Words caught in his throat. The apology he desperately wanted to give was inadequate. Nothing he could ever say or do would be enough.

"Why *did* you come? Did you have to see for yourself?" Ron Redecke asked in an even tone. He held his hand over the mounded earth. "There they are. There's my wife and my children. There's my entire life, everything I ever loved."

"Sir, I know you're hurt—" Joan Chadwell began, stepping forward to shield her son.

"Please, just go away," Ron Redecke said. He turned away from them, pulling his children with him.

"I'm sorry," Alex managed through the emotion choking him. Tears burned his eyes but he refused to let them fall.

The man stopped. He stared at the drying grass for a long moment. Finally, he looked up and over the quiet cemetery.

"My babies are gone. And the woman that—" the man's voice failed him and he took a shuddering breath.

"—the woman that I love is gone. And you're sorry?" he demanded. Alex bowed his head. The breathtaking guilt was crushing him. He waited for more words, more hate and condemnation. When Ron Redecke said no more, Alex looked up. The man's face was a battleground. Anger and sadness fought for control of him. For a moment, Alex recognized another emotion in the man's eyes. For just a second compassion shimmered behind the tears.

"It's not your fault. It's not. I know it's not, but you *were* the other driver. And I'll never be able to forget that. I'll never forgive that."

"Dad," Gabriel said quietly. "Dad, let's go."

The three left without another word.

"Alex?"

"What happens now, Mom? What do I do now?" Alex asked in a terrified voice. This was never supposed to happen. How did life continue after this?

"I don't know, Alex. I don't know."

15

Wynn

It had taken Wynn a moment to recognize the young man. She recognized him first as the baseball player and football star, one of the most popular guys in high school. She had been told that it had been a Chadwell that had caused the accident, but she had not associated the two until she saw him there. He had looked so broken, terrified. Why had he come? Why did he feel he had to see them?

Wynn pulled her jacket tighter around her and rested her chin on her arms. Her father's anger had surprised her. She had expected him to be stronger. She had expected him to comfort the boy, to tell him that he forgave him. She had been ready to grow angry at her father for doing what God said to. But he hadn't.

She turned a pebble over and over between her fingertips. The sun was setting. Pools of color seeped across the sky. The clouds were deepening in shades of purple.

"Hiding?"

She did not look up.

"Nope. I knew you'd find me."

Gabriel lowered himself to the wooden step beside her. The house was full of people, but not the people that were supposed to be there.

"I'd give anything to have Caleb here smashing my art project," Wynn whispered. Warm drops clung to her eyelashes but did not fall. Gabriel slipped an arm around her shoulders. They leaned into one another, both silent for many moments. There was nothing to say.

"I miss them, Gabe. It hurts so bad." Wynn breathed in a shuddering breath. "What do we do now?"

Gabriel stared at the ground. Wynn could see a tear trickling down his cheek. Gabriel was crying.

"I don't know, Wynn."

Part Two

Seven years later…

16

Alex tossed the plush football. A skinny youth caught it with ease and sent it spiraling back in his direction.

"So then Howton tackled him. Ended up cracking a rib, but didn't tell anybody 'til the game was over. They won by one touchdown. It was pretty harsh," he said with a shake of his head. Alex flinched.

"Maybe it was a good thing I missed the game after all. Sounds like I would've been brought to tears," he commented. Lydale shrugged and gave the right wheel of his wheelchair a hard turn, adjusting his position.

"Mom yelled at the refs for every call they made. She was mad."

"You're pretty lucky to have a mom who likes football. My mom still hates it and I played from second grade through high school," Alex told the sixteen-year-old. Lydale shrugged again.

"Mr. Alex?"

Alex turned to see a small girl with no hair looking up at him. She swished the skirt of her robe as if it were a princess's ball gown.

"Yes, Miss Dora?"

"I want to watch *Mary Poppins*," she informed him,

holding up a DVD case. Alex reached for the case. Dora relinquished her hold, and grinned hugely.

"*Mary Poppins*," he repeated in his best cockney accent. He turned to Lydale. "'Scuse me, Gov'ner."

"You're crazy," Lydale said. Alex shrugged.

"That hasn't been medically proven yet." He held out a hand to Dora. "Shall we?"

He had to bend so that the six-year-old could reach his finger. She latched on and dragged him toward the media room. Once she stood him in front of the television, she waited patiently for him to start the movie.

"There you go, little lady."

"Will you watch it with me? Pleeeaaaase?" She put on her best pouty face. Alex pulled a pink beanbag chair from the pile by the wall and set it on the floor for her.

"I can't. I have to get to work soon. But here," he said, snatching a three foot tall stuffed bear from the counter, "Rufus will watch it with you. He loves *Mary Poppins*."

"When are you going to be a real doctor?" she asked as he set the bear beside the beanbag. The plush animal fell over and he righted it again. The bear would not sit up straight. Finally, he leaned it against the beanbag, giving its bean-filled nose a whack for being so difficult.

"A real doctor? What do you mean a real doctor?"

"When do you get your heart listening thingie?" she questioned, settling into her chair and pulling Rufus up to sit beside her. Alex scratched his head.

"My heart listening thingie? My stethoscope?"

Dora nodded. Alex smiled. Kids made him laugh.

"Can't I be a doctor without a heart listening thingie?"

She shook her head.

"Well I guess I better be getting one. Where do I get one

at, do you think?" he inquired, pulling a small memo book from his back pocket.

"At the heart listening thingie store, silly."

"Heart listening thingie store," he murmured as he wrote down the name. "Well, I'll have to head over there after work and get me one.

"Have fun watching *Mary Poppins* with Rufus, kiddo."

"Bye, Mr. Alex," she called after him. He grinned to himself as he shoved the notebook into his pocket. He'd have to wear a stethoscope around his neck the next time he came to visit Dora.

"See ya, Lydale."

"Bye, Doc," the young man replied, before wheeling toward the media room. A few other kids waved goodbye as Alex left the cheerful room. One little boy smiled at him from his hospital bed. A nurse checked his feeding tube and then the bag that held his liquid lunch.

"What are you having for lunch today, A.J.?" Alex asked as he passed. The boy looked up at the IV bag full of dietary supplement. It was a game he played. He pretended the bag was filled with good foods that other kids liked to eat but he would never get to taste.

"Chee pia a marmalo a-a-a woobee!" A.J. wheezed.

"Cheese pizza, marshmallows, and root beer?"

The boy grinned and nodded.

"Sounds great. You're making me hungry," he told him, clutching his stomach. A.J. gave a wheezy laugh and then answered a question the nurse asked him.

Alex snatched his lab coat off the hook at the entrance and turned the corner, nearly colliding with a group of nursing students.

"Oh, pardon me." He offered a smile and continued on

down the hall.

Half of the young women turned to stare after the tall man.

"And that is another benefit of being a nurse," DeJanna Watkins said with a coy smile

"Keep your minds on your work, ladies," an older woman named Patty reprimanded. She let a smile slip out as she shook her head. "Come on."

"Was he a doctor?" a short blonde questioned as the group began to move again.

"He's in his first year of residency," Patty obliged. "Now focus, ladies."

She led the women to the nurses' station and explained their assignments.

Several hours later, all the women but one were gathering their things to leave.

"Where's the other one?" Patty asked of the earthen-skinned DeJanna. The pretty, young woman shrugged.

"I haven't seen her since our break."

"She was with that little Daugherty girl in 127," April Potts offered as she snatched a peppermint from a candy dish lying on the counter.

"Thanks. Good job today girls," Patty said as she made a note on her clipboard and then started off down the hall. The girls chattered noisily as they discussed dinner plans and headed for the exit.

Patty still had a few hours more to go before she was able to leave. Her feet hurt and her back hurt, but the day had gone well so far. She enjoyed working with the students, but sometimes they wore on her nerves. She stopped just outside of Dora Daugherty's door and looked in.

"And then they flew right up the chimney!" Dora said,

holding her blanket aloft to demonstrate.

"Well, how did they do that?" asked a young woman wearing a lavender t-shirt under her white scrubs. She sat in a chair next to the little girl's hospital bed.

"It just sucked them up," Dora made a slurping sound, "and then spit them out." She demonstrated this as well.

"Wow! That's amazing. Mary Poppins would be a pretty neat person to have around, huh?"

"Oh, yeah, but she's just pretend. Mommy told me so. Sometimes I pretend like I'm Jane and Patrick, he's my brother, he likes to be Michael. Maybe you could be Mary Poppins sometime," Dora suggested with a bright smile. Her new friend showed great enthusiasm.

"That would be lots of fun."

"Ahem," Patty interrupted, dramatically clearing her throat and stepping into the room. Two heads popped up.

"Mrs. Pool. I told Dora's mother I would sit with Dora while she ran down to the cafeteria," the nurse-in-training quickly explained.

"I see. I'd like to speak with you as soon as Mrs. Daugherty returns," Patty informed the young woman.

"Miss Patty, I think you would be a good Katy-Nanna," Dora said. The young woman at Dora's side covered her mouth with both hands. Just then, a flustered Mrs. Daugherty returned with a styrofoam Gold Star box and three cups of coffee.

"They didn't have hamburgers! The one night I'm cravin' a cheeseburger and there's not a beef patty to be found! Just my luck.

"Thank you for staying with her. You're a real sweetheart. Dora I brought you a chocolate chip cookie." The little blustery woman cast a glance at Patty. "You should hire her on full time, you know. Dora, say bye to the nice lady."

"Bye-bye," Dora said with a smile and a wave.

"Bye, Dora. You have a good night. I hope you have a nice evening, Mrs. Daugherty," replied the 'nice lady'. She stepped around Patty and then waited for her outside.

"I'm sorry. I—" she started as soon as Patty shut the door.

"For what? I didn't come find you to yell at you." Patty studied the tall young woman. She looked frightened and Patty nearly laughed. Short, round Patty Pool seldom struck fear into the hearts of young people.

"You've done a good job all three times that you've been here. A real good job. Are you wanting to be a pediatric nurse or are you still considering the options?"

"Yes. I mean yes I plan to be a pediatric nurse."

"Gwyneth, isn't it? Have you got a job?" Patty inquired, starting back toward the nurses' station. The student fell into step beside her.

"Wynn. Everyone calls me Wynn. I'm an STNA at a nursing home, but I'm looking for another job," Wynn announced, rather excitedly. Her green eyes sparkled at the prospects of a job at the Children's Hospital.

"Stop by the Human Resource center tomorrow and fill out an application. I'll talk to the lady who does the hiring and tell her I want you here."

Wynn was nearly jumping up and down.

"Oh, thank you! Thank you so much. This is so, so, so . . . this is great!"

Patty smiled at the young woman's enthusiasm. They needed a few more kids like her.

"Now, go on and get studying or partying or whatever

it is you do on a Friday night," she commanded. Wynn chuckled.

"Tonight I go to the grocery store, go to the laundromat, study while my clothes are washing, go home and study some more."

"Sounds like fun."

"Oh, yes. Thanks again, Mrs. Pool. I really appreciate this," Wynn said as she gathered her sweatshirt from behind the desk. Patty waved her off and the young woman nearly skipped down the hall.

"Hey, Patty Pool. How're you this evening?" a deep voice suddenly asked from behind her. Patty turned to see a young doctor approaching. She shrugged.

"It's been a pretty good day. I just got rid of all the nursing students for the day," she told him with a mock sigh of relief. The doctor reached for a patient's file. He was working this week under one of the surgeons and was completing rounds to check up on the attending's patients.

"They couldn't be that bad."

"No, no, they're all pretty good. I want the one that just left to work here. Real sweet thing. Pretty, too," she added, glancing over at him. The young man nodded absently.

"I think you'd like her."

His head popped up and his eyes narrowed. "Oh, no you don't. The last time I let one of you set me up with a girl, I ended up taking an English major who never shut up to the movies. It was the worst evening of my life. Uh-uh."

"English major? Who set you up?" Patty questioned on a laugh.

"Dr. Dornhecker set me up with her niece. And the time before that it was a fellow resident who loved the opera. Have you ever been to an opera? Well I went to four before

I got smart and stopped asking her out," he answered, returning to the file. Patty shrugged. She had never been much of a matchmaker anyway.

"I'm going to check on Gordon Goss and pop in on Dora. She gets to go home tomorrow and she has to see me with a stethoscope so she'll think I'm a real doctor," Alex told her, gesturing toward the instrument hanging around his neck. Patty gathered the medicine charts and nodded.

"She asked me yesterday if I was a real nurse. She said I didn't wear a white dress and a funny hat."

"She's a cute kid," Alex said as they started down the hall together.

"Yeah. They all are. Well, have fun, Doctor. I'm off to do more paperwork."

Alex waved over his head as he walked on. Patty smiled to herself. He was a good kid. The hospital needed to hang onto him.

17

Wynn slung her bag over her shoulder, piled grocery bags into her heaping laundry basket, and slammed the trunk of her car. Groaning, she hefted the heavy basket and lumbered toward the apartment building. She did a high kick and hit the doorbell with the toe of her white shoe.

"Yes?"

"Ash, it's me. Can you come let me in and get some more of these groceries from my trunk?" she asked the metal box in the wall.

"I'll be right down. I have to get my shoes on," her roommate replied. Wynn waited semi-patiently, humming "Jingle Bells" as the load grew heavier. Finally, the metal door swung open and Ashleigh Osman stood to the side to let her pass.

"I couldn't find my tennis shoes," she said explaining the delay in her arrival. Wynn glanced down at her feet and laughed. Ashleigh was standing on two-inch heels.

"Oh. Here, my keys are in my pocket," she announced, turning sideways so Ashleigh could reach in the pouch of her scrubs for her keys. Ashleigh slid a rock in front of the door.

"Hold the elevator. I'll be right back."

Wynn shifted the heavy load and struggled to the elevator. She pushed the button with the corner of her basket. The door opened just as Ashleigh came rushing in laden with groceries.

"So, guess what. Never mind. You'll never guess. I found the perfect dress today. You'll absolutely love it. It wasn't too bad either. Four hundred and fifty. That's pretty cheap, you know. And I've finally decided on the bridesmaids' color. It's called baby powder pink. It's so pretty. I'm having yours made white with pink trim. White will kinda' set you apart, since you're the maid of honor, you know? Now I just have to choose the pattern," Ashleigh rambled, as they stepped on. She punched the fourth floor button with her long, silver-tipped fingernail. Wynn set the basket against the handrail and sagged against the lime green wall. Ashleigh hummed a few bars of "Baa Baa Black Sheep" before suddenly remembering what she had been talking about.

"I can't wait for you to see this dress. It's gorgeous! These heels kill. Ah, my feet hurt. This is why I never wear them. Did you remember to get toilet paper?"

Wynn nodded and hid a smile. The elevator creaked as the motion ceased. The bell dinged

"Did I tell you I've found an internship? Well, I have. At the museum. I'm really excited about it. Go on through. I'll hold the door," Ashleigh volunteered, putting a hand out to hold open the elevator door.

"I got a job tonight," Wynn announced during Ashleigh's momentary silence.

"You did? Wynn, that's fantastic! That's great! Wonderful!"

Ashleigh's oozing enthusiasm was contagious and Wynn laughed.

"Ashleigh, you make the world a happy place."

Ashleigh shrugged. "I do my best. So where is this new job?"

Their red apartment door was propped open with a coffee can half full of rocks. Wynn quirked an eyebrow.

"Yeah, yeah, I know. I shouldn't leave the door propped

open, but Ducky's here," Ashleigh excused her lack of caution. "So where's the job?"

Wynn kicked the door open wider, and stepped over the door prop and into the tiny living room.

"Children's."

The linoleum floor was covered with bright throw rugs and she tripped over a green one lying near the door.

"Let me help you, Wynn," Octavia Duckworth offered from the couch. She pushed a stack of books to the side and ran to assist in unloading the groceries.

"Children's? Wynn, that really is great. It's perfect for you," Ashleigh commented, already searching through the grocery bags. Wynn handed off some of her load and thanked her second roommate.

"Yeah, no problem.

"Ash, Ben called. Said to give him a ring when you get in," the British, brunette announced as she hefted the plastic bags. The women dropped their loads on the countertop and small café table in the tiny kitchen. Ashleigh found a package of gummy bears and her eyes lit up.

"I'm going to go call him. And I'm stealing these gummy bears."

Wynn fetched the toilet tissue and bottle of shampoo from a bag and tossed them at Ashleigh. "Be a dear and put these away as you go by."

Ducky started unloading the bags nearest her. She nonchalantly tucked her long hair behind her ears.

"Oh yeah, your brother called, too. He's going to stop by for a bit after eight. I told him to be a good chap and pick up a pizza. Said he would. He's such a sweet bloke."

Wynn smiled. Gabe would stand on his head if Ducky asked him to. He was enamored with the sophomore

Conservatory student and had been since they had met.

"Sweet on you, maybe," Wynn quipped with a teasing smile, as she placed a jar of spaghetti sauce in a cabinet. Ducky gave her a dubious look.

"Oh, go on."

Wynn shrugged and tossed a loaf of bread in her direction. She opened the refrigerator to put away a package of sliced turkey breast and pulled out a container full of molding casserole.

"Yum, yum." She wrinkled her nose and dropped the covered bowl in the sink.

"It was Ashleigh's turn to clean the refrigerator," Ducky suggested, flinging open the blue painted cabinet door and shoving in a box of Whole Grain O's .

There was a knock on the door and Wynn glanced at her watch. He was fifteen minutes early.

"Delivery boy," Gabe called from the other side. Wynn made no move to answer the door. She smiled sweetly at her roommate.

"I'll get it," Ducky finally said with sarcastic enthusiasm. Once Gabe was let into the room, he greeted the occupants and handed the pizzas off to his sister.

"One loaded and, just for you, a mushroom and olive," he told her, slipping out of his jacket. Wynn set the boxes on the counter and reached for plates.

"You were right, Ducky. He really is a sweet bloke," she imitated. Ducky's oval face turned rosy, but she chuckled.

"He'd be sweeter if he'd picked up a pint from Graeters."

Gabe pulled a paper sack from his book satchel. "I got that raspberry, chocolate chip stuff."

The women stared at him in disbelief and he smiled.

"How did you know I'd want ice cream?" Ducky

demanded.

"I'm a psychology major, ladies. It's Friday, nearly midterms, and you're stressed out. Obviously, you need some form of comfort. It's a well known fact that ice cream is a comfort food. Graeters is your favorite brand of ice cream and Wynn loves that raspberry stuff. You see? It's elementary, my dear Watson," Gabe explained, tossing open the lid to the pizza box.

"Well, I'm impressed," Ducky conceded, pulling a pitcher of Kool-Aid from the refrigerator.

"Bless you, Gabriel Redecke," Wynn said staring lovingly at the pint of ice cream. Gabriel piled four slices of pizza onto a plate while she placed the ice cream in the freezer.

"Gabe, would you like some?" Ducky asked, gesturing toward the pitcher.

"Yeah. Thanks."

Wynn suddenly threw her arms around her brother's neck and gave him a kiss on the cheek. "You're the bestest brother in the whole wide world."

Gabriel looked at his twin as if she had suddenly lost her mind. "You're really weird."

18

Alex loosened his tie and tossed it onto the back of his couch while a three-month-old Labrador jumped around at his feet.

"Hey, Busby. Come on let's go out," he greeted the squirming, ball of fur. He opened the back door and let the dog into the tiny back yard. He returned to the kitchen and hit the button on the answering machine on the counter. As the machine announced the number of new messages, he began to scour the fridge for leftovers.

"Chadwell, it's Porter. How about a game on Sunday afternoon? We're meeting at the park at two. Give me a call."

"Hello, Mr. Chadwell. My name is Ardua Padua with Master Card. We were reviewing your account and have noticed that your payment is five days overdue. Please return my call as quickly as possible so that we might rectify this situation," said a heavily accented voice. The woman then left her phone and extension number. Alex paused in his search.

"I sent that check off last week," he told the machine. He let the refrigerator door shut on its barren interior.

"Alex ? Are you there? Well, of course you're not. You're at work. I was just wondering what you were doing on Saturday. Your dad is flying to New York this weekend. I thought I might drive up to Cincinnati to see you. I could shop while you're working. I'd come up tomorrow morning and I'll leave Monday morning. You just let me know. And be honest if you don't want me to come. I'm baking some cookies right now. And you thought I couldn't cook. Oh, they're burning! I've got to go."

Alex smiled and shook his head as the message ended. Glancing around his small kitchen, he noticed how bare the cabinets were. He hated grocery shopping almost as much as he hated laundry, but he would need to do both soon. *And wash the dishes*, he mentally added, noting the pile of dirtied plates overflowing in the sink. He shrugged out of his blazer and threw it over a chair. He hated dressing up. He would be glad when he got to work the emergency room rotation and could wear scrubs. He pulled his shirttail out of his slacks and grabbed a Pepsi from the refrigerator. Busby was scratching on the backdoor. His landlord would be angry when he saw the rips Busby had put in the screen. The dog ran past him toward his bowl and noisily lapped up some water.

Alex left the kitchen and fell into the overstuffed recliner that sat in a prime position in front of the television. The chair had been a rare find and had served him well through his college years. He had discovered it on the side of the road awaiting the arrival of the garbage collectors. His mother had been trying to replace it with a new one for years now, but Alex firmly refused. This was his game-watching chair. This was a man's chair.

He reached for the remote but his hand encountered the cordless phone instead. Busby suddenly ran and took a flying leap, landing hard against his stomach.

"Guess I might as well be a good friend and son and return my phone calls," he muttered to the dog, who decided to clean Alex's face.

"Hey now! Aw, come on. Your breath smells. Shoo, you need to brush your teeth." He pushed the dog's face away and Busby finally settled down. Dialing Rick Porter's number, he kicked off his shoes and popped the tab on his Pepsi can. Rick did not answer so Alex left a message on his voicemail, agreeing to the proposed softball game. His mom answered on the second ring.

"Hey, Mom."

"Alex?"

"Who else would be calling you 'mom'?" Alex quipped as he searched the cushions for the remote.

"Well, it might have been someone with the wrong number. Did you get my message? Well of course you got my message. Why else would you call?"

"I got your message. Bring some of those cookies with you tomorrow."

"I would, but I forgot to add the sugar and didn't realize until I gave some to little Gus Turner next door. He told me they tasted like dog biscuits.

"Oh, you want me to come? Really?" she asked, sounding a bit unsure.

"Of course I want you to come, Mom. You know you can visit anytime you want."

"I know how busy you are. I don't want to interrupt your plans."

Alex's hand closed around the remote control. He wrestled it from between the cushions. "I have no plans, but a softball game on Sunday. I have the weekend off. I planned to laze around and do absolutely nothing."

"Perfect. I can spoil you for the weekend. Well, I'm going to start packing right now. I'll see you tomorrow. Love you. Bye." The phone line went dead before Alex could reply. He looked at his dog who had laid his head on his paws.

"This is perfect timing, Buzz. Mom'll go to the grocery

store for me, do my laundry, and wash my dishes. She should visit every week."

Alex scratched the dog between the ears as hunger pangs hit.

"Well, Boy, I'm about to starve to death. How does pizza sound?" he asked, making use of the speed dial. Busby rolled over so that Alex could scratch his stomach.

"Giovanni's. Will this be pick up or delivery?"

"Delivery. I need a medium mushroom and olive pizza."

19

Wynn picked a mushroom and an olive from her pizza and popped them into her mouth.

"I want you to read over my Psych paper before you go tonight," she told her brother.

"Aren't you afraid I'll spill something on it," he asked around a mouthful. Wynn chuckled at the memory.

"You'll just have to reprint it if you do,"

Ducky stole another piece from a box. "So how's everything going, Mr. Psychology major?" she asked him.

Gabriel started to reply when Ashleigh entered the kitchen with her cell phone at her ear. He paused as all the attention shifted to Ashleigh's one-sided phone conversation.

"No, you're the cutest. Oh, pizza! No, Gabe brought pizza. Yeah, Wynn's brother. Yup. Nope. No. Yeah. Yeah. Uh-uh. No, he has a thing for Ducky," Ashleigh told her fiancé as she loaded a plate full of pizza and poured herself a glass of Kool-Aid. "Pepperoni. I know. No. Yeah, she likes him, but doesn't like him, like him. Well at least she says she doesn't, but I think she does. She probably would if he'd just ask her. Yeah. Um-hmm. Um-hmm." She exited the room with a small wave at everyone. Gabriel and Ducky stared after her in baffled amusement. Gabe's ears were pink and Ducky's face warmed in embarrassment. Wynn looked at Ducky and both of them burst into laughter.

"Oh my. If she weren't so funny, I would hurt her," Ducky said in reference to her blonde roommate. Wynn shook her head and giggled again. Gabe was trying his best not to look uncomfortable. He stuffed his mouth full of pizza.

"I think on that most embarrassing note, I'll go to my room to finish my homework," Ducky announced with a half smile. She glanced at Gabe.

"Thank you for bringing dinner by and the ice cream. If I don't see you before you leave, good night."

Gabe's mouth was still full and he helplessly nodded his farewell. Ducky hid a smile, gathered her plate and books, and disappeared down the hall. Seconds later, they could hear her hissing at Ashleigh. Gabe swallowed and looked at his sister.

"That went well," he sarcastically observed. Wynn chuckled and reached for her cup. "Ashleigh does have a big mouth, but I think she did that on purpose. Trying to help you along a little. Why don't you just ask her out? Ducky, I mean," she suggested before taking a sip.

"Yeah. She seemed real receptive to the idea."

Wynn waved the comment away. "She was embarrassed, that's all."

Gabe shrugged. "She'd never say yes anyway. She's beautiful and talented and is going to be a famous soprano."

"And you're good looking and smart and your future doesn't look too shabby either. Looks to me like a good match," Wynn told him.

"This conversation is officially ended. Change the subject," her brother commanded. His ears were pink again. Wynn smiled. She so enjoyed embarrassing her brother.

"I got a new job today."

"Really? Where?"

"Cincinnati Children's. Well I don't actually have the job yet, I have to apply tomorrow. But one of the nurses said she'd put in a good word for me," she explained.

"That's great. You're training to be a pediatric nurse. It's what you wanted. I'm glad for you."

A siren suddenly broke through the windows. The sound faded as the police car sped away. Gabe glanced toward the window but made no move to check outside.

"I talked to Dad today."

Wynn blinked at the change in subject. "How was he?"

Gabe's green eyes were sad. He shrugged.

"He's the same as always. He talked about the weather and how the pigs were doing. He's gotten a cow. He's nursing her with a bottle. I mentioned something about you and me singing in church and he clammed up." He picked at his pizza and sighed.

"I don't know, Wynn. I don't know if he's ever going to get better. Maybe this is just the way he's going to be."

Wynn swirled the liquid in her cup and watched the ice float in circles. She did not speak for a few long moments.

"It's been seven years. I know he's still angry. Sometimes I'm still angry." She looked up.

"I miss them. There are so many times I say to myself, 'I wish they were here for this. I wish they could see this'. But life goes on. It didn't end for us."

Gabe nodded but said nothing. It had been hard for him. It had taken years for him to let the anger go, but he had come the furthest. Wynn knew she still had a long way to go. In the beginning, she had been furious with God, with herself, her father, and Alexander Chadwell. Depression had set in months after the accident. She had blamed herself, remembering all the times she had been impatient with her brother and sisters, disrespectful to her mother. The emotional rollercoaster ride of guilt and anger had lasted until her freshman year of college. Ashleigh had convinced her to begin going to church again. She began seeing a counselor. She began praying again. She had not forgotten what had happened, but she had finally accepted it.

"Are you happy, Gabe?"

She looked up at him when he did not immediately answer. A small smile stretched over his face.

"Yeah. Yeah, I guess I am. Are you?"

"I am happy with where I'm at and what I am right now, but I don't want to stay here, this way. Make sense?" she wondered. He nodded.

"Perfect sense."

"Daddy's not happy. He's not a hog farmer. He's a preacher. My goodness, have you ever listened to him with the pigs? He lectures them. And he talks to the soybeans. 'You're going to grow into an excellent crop this year'," she mimicked, her voice low and thundering. Gabe chuckled.

"But they listen. He hasn't had a bad crop yet," he said before growing serious.

"I think Papaw Red is sorry he ever offered Dad the farm. It's the perfect excuse. He works from sunup to sundown and never gives himself time to think. But I don't know what to do about it, Wynn."

Wynn nodded. She didn't know what to do either. The man that her father had become was so different from what he had once been. The young, happy-go-lucky, and humorous minister was gone.

"You want to take a trip down to see him soon? Hey, I'm free this weekend, if you are. Felicity scheduled me for next Monday, Tuesday, and Friday night shift instead of giving me the weekend like I asked for," she told him. Gabe pondered the suggestion.

"I am supposed to tutor tomorrow, but Hannah probably won't mind if I cancel. She'll probably be relieved. Let's do it. I'll come pick you up at eight tomorrow."

"Could we stop by Children's so I can fill out that application and turn in my resume?"

"Yeah, sure," Gabe replied.

"You're a good guy, Gabriel Redecke," Wynn told her brother. He grinned.

"I know. Now scoop me some ice cream."

20

Rain tapped on the window and the neighbor kids' Saturday morning cartoons could clearly be heard from the other side of the thin townhouse wall. Busby was whining to be let out.

"My one Saturday off in two months! So much for sleeping in," Alex groaned. He threw the cover back and swung his feet over the side. Busby yelped and took off down the stairs and toward the back door. Alex reached for a t-shirt and slipped it over his head. He yawned and ran a hand through his dark curls. Busby barked from the kitchen.

"Yeah, I'm coming," Alex called. He rounded the corner and tripped over a dog toy lying on the landing. He stumbled down the stairs and into the living room. He yelled out when he saw a body sprawled out on his sofa. The body sat up and began to scream. Alex clutched his chest.

"Mother?"

Joan stopped screaming and stared at him. "Yes?"

Alex shook his head in disbelief and stumbled to his chair. He took a deep breath and willed his heart rate to slow. Finally, he looked at his mother.

"What are you doing here so early? Why didn't you wake me?" he demanded. His mother patted her newly dyed hair.

"I couldn't sleep so I left at three this morning. I pulled up about an hour ago and didn't want to wake you, so I let myself in with the key you gave me."

"I didn't give you a key," Alex reminded. A sheepish

look skittered across his mother's face.

"Oh, well. When I helped you move in I had an extra made. You know for emergency purposes." She turned on the leather couch so that she could face him.

"I'm sorry I startled you."

Alex grinned wryly and then chuckled. Busby began to whine louder and scratch at the door.

"I have to let Busby out," Alex excused himself.

"I picked up some bagels," his mother called as he opened the back door. Busby stared at the water dripping from the gutter and whined again. Alex took his foot and nudged the pup out the door.

"You should decorate this place a little better. A couple of nice pictures on the wall. The kitchen would be lovely if you painted it red. You could have a 1950's theme," Joan went on. Alex opened the refrigerator door and pulled out a gallon of orange juice.

"I thought I might go grocery shopping for you this evening. You have nearly nothing in your fridge and your cabinets are empty. Don't you ever eat at home?" she asked. She floated into the kitchen. Alex noticed his empty sink.

"Oh I did the dishes. I'm surprised that didn't wake you up. Busby was jumping around my feet, whining and making an awful racket. I think you should send him to obedience school. Blueberry?" she asked holding up a bagel.

"Uh, thanks."

She dropped the bagel onto a plate she had fetched from the cabinet. Alex sat down on a black and chrome barstool. He scratched the back of his head and looked up to see his mother staring at him.

"What?" he asked, rubbing his face to make sure there was no encrusted drool there. Joan's eyes were misty and her lip quivered. She shook her head and rubbed her hand over the slate bar top.

"I just can't believe it, is all. My baby's a doctor with his own little place. You've come so far. I'm so proud of you. After all you've been through—"

"Mom," Alex said quietly. His mother covered her mouth with her hand. She had been about to mention the accident. The two remained quiet for a few long moments.

"Sometimes I wonder what became of them. Have you ever thought about it?" Alex inquired. His mother sighed.

"I'm sorry I mentioned it, Alex. I didn't mean to."

His blue eyes met hers. "Have you?"

She shrugged her slight shoulders and reached for a cinnamon raisin bagel. "I heard they moved to Hopkins County—to a farm. I heard the father had family out there."

"They'd be seniors, now, in college, if they went."

"Alex," Joan spoke his name quietly and laid an aging hand over her son's. Alex gave her a wry smile.

"I know. There's no use thinking about the past. I just wonder sometimes."

Joan nodded and looked around Alex's bare kitchen. She opened her mouth but hesitated.

"What?" he prompted.

"I looked them up once when I was visiting Mammaw. He has a farm about forty minutes outside of Hopkinsville. The house was small. They were painting it. It was only half done. The kids were still in high school then. I slowed down and watched them paint. They were laughing." She patted Alex's hand. "I know that doesn't make it easier. But if they can laugh, they are healing. I can't tell you to forget what happened or to whom it happened, but forgive yourself for it, Alex. Maybe you could go to church with me Sunday.

All your answers are there."

He pulled his hand away. "You want some coffee? I still have some of that insanely expensive stuff that Dr. Gregory gave me last Christmas."

Alex fetched a gold foil bag from the corner cabinet and pulled the coffee carafe from the brewer. Joan sighed. He looked up.

"I'm working on it, Mom. I know church has helped you get through all this, but I just can't see how it can help me."

Joan said nothing more though Alex could plainly see that she wanted to. Church had never been a part of his life. Nor had it been a part of his mother's until the accident. She had turned to religion to help her through the police investigations and the newspaper reports, Alex's depression and anger, her husband's aloofness. Church had served as her safe haven. Alex was glad she had found that, glad it helped her through the hard times. He, however, could not so easily believe in a God that would let such horrible things happen. He was stronger than that. He was much too logical.

He pulled a coffee filter from the bag and sighed. As annoying and intruding as his mother was, she had always stood by him and supported him. He supposed he owed her.

"I'm meeting the guys for a game at two on Sunday. I'll go to church with you, just because I'm a good son, but I have to be out of there by one. And don't pick one of those hellfire and brimstone places."

Joan beamed. "You really are a good son."

21

Wynn climbed out of her brother's twelve-year-old Mustang and stretched her back. Gabe had made no stops during the four-hour trip and her poor body ached from the cramped quarters.

"Record timing," Gabe said, checking his watch as he climbed out of the driver's seat. He pulled their duffle bags from the back seat and threw the straps over his shoulders. He looked around the spacious farmland. Dried stalks littered the empty fields. Buttermilk-colored pigs, muddied from the recent rain, lazed on the eroding hillside around the back of the barns. The outbuildings and two huge barns looked even grayer than they had the last visit. The tractor and old Ford sat near the diesel pump, awaiting fill-ups. The house looked lonesome sitting on a hill with only an old, flaming Maple to keep it company. Wynn noticed that her grandma's rose bushes were cut back and the honeysuckle brambles were gone.

"Looks like Daddy's been cleaning up the yard," she commented, shutting the car door with a hard push. The vegetable patch had been harvested and the red-brown earth was tilled. The fruit trees were bare except for a few late apples.

"Bet he's down with the sows. He said old Petri had a new litter. Why don't you go on and find him and I'll take our bags to the house," Gabriel suggested. Wynn gave him a knowing look.

"Oh, sure. Send me down to the stinky, baby pig house." She wrinkled her nose at the mere thought of entering the building where her father kept the mothers and their new litters. She loved the tiny piglets, but the warm, closed up space reeked of ammonia and manure. She much preferred the barn where he kept the older piglets. She loved the way the small pigs came curiously to the fence, their pink snouts sniffing the air. The slightest movement sent them squealing toward the back of the barn. She used to wait until they had come close and then shout just to see them run, tumbling over one another, to safety.

Gabe only grinned at her and started toward the sagging farmhouse. She zipped up her jacket and started down the hard-packed path toward the outbuilding. One of the barn cats ran toward her, attempting to rub against her legs, but only succeeding in tripping her. She accidentally stepped on the poor tabby's tail and sent it howling toward the barn.

"I'm sorry, Kitty. I didn't mean to," she called after the offended feline. The cat refused the apology and disappeared into the shadowy barn. Wynn had always liked dogs better. They were much more forgiving. She could only imagine where the dogs were just now.

"Probably lounging on the back porch, the lazy things," she murmured with affection. The two large mutts did not make very good guard dogs. She reached the building, noticing the empty five-gallon buckets sitting beside the door. Her father was probably feeding the sows. She held her breath and pulled open the door. Her father was leaning over one of the stall doors, lifting one of the piglets up by the tail. He looked up and nearly dropped the baby when he saw her.

"Wynn?"

"Hi, Daddy."

"Well, hello Sweetheart. What are you doing here? Why didn't you call?" he demanded, covering the length of the building with four long-legged steps. He reached to hug her and then drew back.

"I'm all dirty," he said, brushing at his flannel shirt. The piglet squealed and wriggled in his arm.

"Is this one of Petri's?" Wynn questioned. She reached for the squirming animal.

"Yup. The old girl had a real good litter. I think this will be her last. I'm sending her off as soon as these little ones are big enough to do without her."

"Poor Petri," Wynn sympathized. She looked around the dank room. There were three sows, each in her own stall with her babies gathered round her.

"To answer your question, we didn't call because we wanted to surprise you. It was a spur of the moment decision," she told her scruffy looking father. He needed a haircut and a shave and it looked to her as if he had lost some more weight. She had never seen him so gaunt.

"We?"

"Mm-hmm. Gabe came too. He drove," she explained, handing him back Petri's piglet. Her father's face wrinkled with a smile.

"That's great. How long can you stay?"

"We'll head out sometime tomorrow afternoon. I'd like to see Grandma and Papaw Red and Grandma Ivy before we go."

"Call 'em up and invite them to dinner tomorrow. We can throw a roast in the Crock-Pot tonight. Hey, I've got a calf," he announced, lowering the piglet back into the stall. "I'm getting ready to feed her if you'd like to see her."

"Sure." Wynn helped gather the feed buckets, gulping in the fresh air. They were quiet as they trekked to the barn. Small pigs neared the fence as they passed, squealing and running when Ron told them to get on. They hung the buckets in the feed room and he pulled the lid off a plastic trash can full of powdered milk.

"Grab me that bottle there," he commanded, pointing to a shelf full of canisters and feeding bottles. Wynn did as she was told. He scooped the powder into the cylinder and filled it with warm water from the spigot. He forced the rubber nipple over the mouth and shook the liquid until there were no more clumps.

"I have her in the paddock. She's only three weeks. Her momma had twins and refused this one," her father explained as they crossed through the dark barn to the paddock on the other side. A small mewling met Wynn's ears before she spotted the small charcoal head.

"She's so cute!" The calf ran toward them on spindly legs. Her cries grew louder when she spotted the bottle.

"Here," Ron said, shoving the bottle toward her. Wynn smiled and jumped the fence. The animal reached for the bottle, latching on and using her tongue to squeeze the milk out.

"Hold it up," Ron instructed.

"There you are. Hey, Dad!" Gabe greeted as he came up from behind them. He slapped his dad on the shoulder.

"Hey, Sport. Welcome home."

"So this is your new pet. What'd you name her?"

Ron shrugged and looked to the calf hungrily sucking on the bottle. "I haven't. Wynn always named the animals."

"What about Podie. There was a little boy at the clinic who had a teddy bear named Podie," Wynn told them, patting the big-eyed cow between her ears. The calf nudged the nearly empty bottle.

"Works for me," Ron shrugged. A smile suddenly broke

on his weathered face.

"It's good to have you both home. I think this calls for a celebration. I'll finish up the chores and get cleaned up. I'm taking y'all out to supper." He patted Gabe on the shoulder and then lumbered off to finish feeding the animals. Gabe waited until he was out of earshot, then sighed.

"He's like an old man, Wynn," he said, staring after his forty-six year old father. Wynn nodded. He had aged twenty years in the past seven. Wynn pulled the empty bottle away from Podie and handed it to her brother. The calf pushed against her side, wanting more.

"He's a skeleton."

Gabe said nothing. He distracted Podie while Wynn climbed over the fence.

"It makes it harder."

Gabriel put a hand on her shoulder. "God knows what he needs, Wynn. He sees him."

Wynn puffed out her cheeks. "Seeing Daddy makes it hard to believe in God."

22

Alex felt conspicuous as he entered the church foyer. He felt as though he had a sign over his head that said UNBELIEVER in flashing red lights. People milled through the room and laughter sounded from every corner. The smiles that were sent his way seemed genuine, but he felt as if they were biding their time, waiting for the opportune moment to pounce on him and beat him over the head with their black Bibles. He followed his mother to a padded pew near the back and sat down. The sanctuary was painted a cream color and contemporary stained glass windows gave him plenty to look at. Large chandeliers dangled from the ceiling. Alex noted that if the lamps were to fall he and his mother would be knocked out by one of the curved brass arms.

"Thank you, Alex, for coming," his mother said from beside him. She looked toward the ceiling. "What are you looking at?"

He grinned. "Nothing."

His mother looked confused and then gave a slight shrug. She smoothed her pale green skirt and glanced at the pulpit. The phone book had said that this church preached the fundamental truths. She hoped the pastor was not too lively. She did not want her son scared away.

Alex unbuttoned his suit coat and opened the bulletin he had been handed. He chuckled.

"What?"

He pointed to the printed words. "They have a schedule." He had never thought of a church service being run on a schedule.

A stooped, old lady suddenly hobbled up.

"Welcome to Living Branch. I'm Clara Beetle," she greeted reaching out a knotted, blue-veined hand.

"Alex Chadwell," Alex returned, as he shook the elderly woman's hand. He touched his mother's shoulder. "This is my mother, Mrs. Joan Chadwell."

"Wonderful to meet you, Ms. Beetle," Joan smiled broadly.

"Are you new to the area?" the inquisitive Clara Beetle wanted to know.

"I'm visiting my son. I live in western Kentucky."

"Do tell. What part?"

"Morganfield in Union County."

"Why I was born in Corydon. That isn't but a stone's throw from Morganfield. My husband's brother still lives down there," Clara told them. She scooted forward and continued speaking with Joan while a host of other parishioners strode up to say hello. By the time the flood of greeters stemmed, Alex had introduced himself a dozen times.

"Friendly folk, I'll give you that," he whispered to his mother as the praise band stepped to their microphones. She smiled at him. A tall, brunette with an amazing voice and a British accent called the congregation to worship. Alex spent the next twenty minutes paying more attention to her than to the words or rhythms of the songs. Finally, Joan nudged him.

"The words're that way," she whispered, pointing to the screen on which the words were projected. Alex grinned at her and dutifully studied the screen.

Once the songs ended, the announcements had been made, and the guitar player had prayed, a short, ruddy-faced man stepped to the pulpit.

"Good morning all. Welcome back for another blessed Sunday. I got up this morning and was happy to see the sun shining. How about you?" The man waited for nods and amens before continuing. "We have a few visitors this morning. I want to personally welcome you to Living Branch Fellowship. I'm Leo Polk, senior pastor here."

"Now if you'll all turn in your Bibles to Genesis, chapter thirty-seven. We're continuing our study of the patriarchs and today we move onto Joseph." He flipped open his thin Bible and arranged his notes. He rubbed his hands together and gave his congregation a moment to find their place in the Scriptures.

"Now Joseph went through many trials and tribulations. At first glance you may wonder, why him? He did nothing to deserve all this."

Alex settled into the pew, hoping this preacher was not too long-winded. He had planned to take his mother to lunch before returning her to the townhouse and meeting up with the guys. He cast a glance toward the brunette and the group of young adults she sat with. Joan poked him in the side when she noticed his mind was drifting. He turned his attention back to Pastor Polk.

"Now, I don't know if you ever noticed, but Joseph was something of a spoiled brat. Just look. He was the first son of Rachel and Jacob and the Bible says that Jacob loved him more than his other sons. He made Joseph a special coat." He straightened his own suit coat for emphasis. Alex fidgeted with a paper clip he found in his pants pocket. His mother pinched his arm.

"Then Joseph starts having these dreams in which he is ruling over all his brothers. He tells his brothers about these dreams. I imagine him gloating, rubbing it in. That doesn't make his brothers too happy." The pastor smiled and nodded knowingly.

"Now, I have four younger brothers and by the time Cory, the youngest, came along, my folks were too tired to do much with him. They spoiled him, let him have his way a lot. It was left up to me and my other brothers to instill the fear of God into Cory. Believe you me, if he had done like Joseph, we would have sold him off too.

"Joseph was just seventeen years old when his brothers sold him into slavery. He was young, beloved of his father, and strong. I imagine Joseph was a bit full of himself. But God chose to use him. He didn't choose him because he was young or well liked or strong. He chose him because Joseph needed God." He paused. "Let me repeat that. God chose Joseph because Joseph needed God. He was imperfect, full of sin. God took him and allowed these tribulations to happen because he was shaping him. Joseph needed to be pruned so that he could grow. Now let's look at what exactly our boy Joseph went through."

Alex had never heard the story of Joseph before. He knew the Christmas story and the Easter story and that was the extent of his biblical knowledge. But this story intrigued him. As the pastor related the events of the young man's life, Alex was drawn in.

"God took a young, strong man and allowed him to be made weak. He brought him about as low as he could go. But when Joseph was at his lowest, when he was humble and knew he couldn't do it on his own, God lifted him up. He made him stronger than he ever could have been on his own. He used him to save two nations, his own family, and, in reality, the Jewish and Christian faiths. You see what God can do? He can take all of these horrible events and turn them around. He can use them for good. It says in Romans 'that all things work together for good to those who love God'. God's big enough to even use our mistakes and our shortcomings. Isn't that good to know?"

Alex shifted in his seat. Was it his imagination or did Pastor Polk look directly at him when quoting that Scripture?

The sermon continued. Pastor Polk quoted many more Scriptures, related histories, and interspersed his lesson with well-chosen anecdotes. Finally, he concluded with a challenge.

"Beloved, when God allows you to go through these hard times he doesn't leave you alone. He's not an evil, cruel God that wants you to have a difficult life. He does not require humility because He delights in seeing you weak. No. God knows that it's only when we are weak that we can rely on Him and on our Christian brothers and sisters. It's only in this unity, this interdependence on our God and our heavenly family, that we can ever be strong enough to make it through this difficult life.

"Beloved, is God pruning you? Is He growing you into the person He wants you to be? Into the person you were meant to be? Let me beg you not to try and go through these hard times alone. Don't think you are invincible. We need one another and we need God." The pastor closed his Bible.

The keyboardist began playing softly as he offered an altar call. Alex stood with everyone else, gripping the wooden back of the pew in front of him. He had no desire to know this God, or to allow Him to weaken him. He had been through the greatest trial of his life and survived it without the help of a god. He was doing just fine.

23

Wynn curled her feet under her on the blue gingham sofa and told of the job Patty had offered her. Her grandparents sat dispersed around the room. They had been surprised at their grandchildren's unexpected arrival and had immediately agreed to travel to the farm for a Sunday lunch. Grandma Red had arrived with a golden loaf of sourdough bread and an orange juice cake, Wynn's favorite. Grandma Ivy had entered the house bearing baked goods for the "kids" to take back to school with them.

"Sounds like a good job, Baby Doll," Papaw Red said in reference to Wynn's announcement. He sipped his coffee and looked to Gabe.

"What have you been up to lately?"

Gabe shrugged. "I'm working on my senior project. Right now I am conducting a survey concerning grief."

Eyes involuntarily turned toward Ron Redecke. He was staring out the window, paying little attention to the conversation. Gabe continued.

"I'm still working as Dr. Alcott's assistant and in the clinic on the weekends. And being a resident assistant takes up a lot of time. I'm always barking out orders or planning a program. I'm jealous that Wynn has her own place."

The next onslaught of questions was for Wynn.

"How's the apartment?" "How're your roommates?" "Are you taking care of yourself?" "Do you have enough food?"

She answered them all with a smile and the conversation swiftly moved on. Wynn kept an eye on her withdrawn father. The large windows poured light into the room, but he had chosen the shadowy corner. He sat in the easy chair with a cup of coffee on the table beside him. He had said little over lunch and even less since. He seemed to always be distracted. Even now he stared into space.

Wynn glanced around, wondering what her father's blank eyes had fastened on. The family photos that Wynn had had sitting around the bright living room were gone now. The walls were bare. He had sent all her mother's things with her when she left home. Caleb and Chassity and Hope's things were packed in boxes and stored in the attic. There was nothing left in the house to remind him of his family. This was how he dealt with life now. He forgot it. He buried it.

"Wynn, Hon?"

Wynn looked up to see her brother and grandparents staring at her. She felt her cheeks warming.

"I'm sorry."

"Oh, don't you worry about it. Papaw was just teasing you anyways," Grandma Red told her, patting Wynn's knee.

"I was just askin' ya if ya had any fellers up there in Cincinnati."

Wynn laughed. Her last 'feller' had been Jeremy Ritter, the captain of their high school debate team and valedictorian of their class. He had headed off to UCLA and she had gone to Cincinnati. The two of them were still good friends but laughed at the thought of a future together.

"I'm too busy for 'fellers', Papaw. Besides I need to get myself straightened out before I start shopping for one."

Grandma Ivy smiled softly. She knew that Wynn was still working things through. She was proud of her for it. She reached over to squeeze Wynn's hand and Wynn squeezed right back. Grandma Ivy was praying for her, was praying for them all. And that helped more than she knew.

24

"Well, well, look who's here. Hey boys, Dr. Chadwell has come at last," Rick Porter announced as Alex jogged over the spongy ground toward the baseball diamond. The group of men began to cheer outrageously.

"I told you I'd be here," he said, throwing his bag onto a metal bench.

"Good to see you, Buddy," Porter said with a grin, giving him a backslapping hug. A few of the other men yelled out greetings.

"Hey, Chadwell. Nice of ya to join us. What's been keeping ya?" Jimmy Kimball called from where he was tying on his cleats. It had been a while since Alex had been able to make it to their weekly softball games. He looked around at them all. These were the guys he'd gone through college with. Now they were quickly becoming out-of shape businessmen and accountants. One was a reporter. Jimmy was a loan officer. Two were still in medical school. Porter was in law school. A few of them were married. Steve Perch was expecting his second kid.

Alex pulled the baseball cap from his back pocket and pushed it onto his head.

"Responsibilities, man. Residency's rough. Being a doctor's harder than it looks on TV," he said with a shrug.

"Yeah, life stinks. I want to go back to college," Brandon Hunter said, pulling a catcher's mitt from his bag.

"I'm surprised you even remember college, Hunter. You were usually too drunk to stand up."

Hunter grinned. "That's what I loved about it. Chadwell and I used to have a contest on who could get the best test score after a six-pack. This man's brilliant even with a hangover." He put an arm around Alex's neck. Alex grinned half-heartedly and shrugged him off.

"So who are we playing?" Alex changed the subject, flexing his glove. Porter shrugged and slid on a pair of mirrored sunglasses.

"Some church team. They wanted to scrimmage. Surprised they agreed to a Sunday practice."

"A church team?" Alex repeated.

"Yeah. So easy on the language, Boys," Porter cautioned certain members of the team. Steve swung a bat at an invisible ball.

"I've been asking you to clean up your foul mouths for years," he reminded, adjusting his stance for another immaterial pitch. Steve was a tall, husky man, built like a tank. He was a police officer now and could probably snap the rest of them in two. When they were all still undergrads they had called Steve the preacher. He was the only religious one among them. He had never gone to the parties or been as obnoxious as the rest of them. He had quietly and inoffensively taken a stand. They all had respected him for that, but had never felt compelled to join him at his weekly Bible studies.

"Yeah, but we never listen to you," Hunter threw out. Steve rolled his eyes.

"Yeah, if you had you would all be good, upstanding citizens by now. But my words fall on deaf ears."

"Not all. Look at Dr. Chadwell, here. Have you ever seen a more upstanding citizen?" Jimmy asked, throwing an arm around Alex's neck and punching him in the shoulder. "Pediatric doctor, free-clinic volunteer, all-around do-gooder. And to top it all off he's been sober for years now."

Alex took the good-natured ribbing with a grin.

"Yeah, I even took my mother to church this morning and made time to hang out with my old college buddies," he replied with an arrogant shrug.

Hunter shuddered. "You've turned into what none of us ever wanted to be."

"What's that?"

"An adult."

A few of the guys laughed. Steve reached over to slap Alex on the back.

"Welcome to the club, man."

"Looks like our worthy opponents have arrived," Porter said, waving over a group of uniformed ballplayers. Alex looked up expecting to see a group of out-of-shape middle-aged men. That's not what he saw.

"They're going to slaughter us," Jimmy commented rather nonchalantly. Alex nodded in agreement. These men looked like they played for the Major Leagues.

"Hey!" a mountain of a man called out as his team neared. Porter went forward to shake the hand he offered.

"Ben Lee," the man introduced himself. "Thanks for practicing with us."

"Rick Porter. We're glad to do it." The two men introduced the members of their team.

"So's your team got a name?" Ben wanted to know. Steve grinned wryly.

"The Motley Crew," he answered.

"We're 'The Pirates Who Don't Do Anything'," Ben supplied. Steve seemed to know the significance of the name when none of the rest of his teammates did.

"VeggieTales?" he asked with a grin.

Ben nodded toward a man at the back of the group.

"Marquis's four-year-old named us. He's a VeggieTales fan. I hope you don't mind, but our families are coming to watch." He motioned toward a group of women and children just topping the hill. A few of the men shrugged.

"Not a problem," Porter said.

"Great. Then let's play ball."

An hour and a half later, the men gathered on the sidelines to shake hands. Jimmy's prophecy had come true. The Crew had been slaughtered—fifteen to seven.

"You're a good ball player," Ben Lee told Alex as they shook hands. Alex shrugged. He used to be better.

"You've got a good team."

"We all played baseball in college," Ben explained as a petite blonde sidled up to him. He slipped an arm around her.

"You're all sweaty," she objected, as she squirmed out of the crook of his arm. She handed him a can of orange soda.

"Chadwell, isn't it? This is my fiancée, Ashleigh," Ben announced, grinning like a fool. Ashleigh smiled up at him, before extending a slender hand toward Alex.

"It's a pleasure to meet you," he said.

"You too." The pretty, young woman frowned. "You look so familiar. You don't attend the Art Academy, do you?"

Alex shook his head. "No. I attended UC."

"Hmm," she murmured, studying him for a moment longer. Finally, she shrugged and the friendly smile returned.

"If you all ever want someone to scrimmage against again, give me a call," Ben offered.

"How about next Sunday?" Hunter called out. "We used to be the best. We have to win our reputation back."

Ben looked to his teammates who turned to their wives and girlfriends. Most received tolerant nods.

"You've got a game."

25

"It feels so good to be home," Wynn announced, melting into the cardinal red couch cushion. Her body ached from riding in her brother's small car. She had some homework she needed to finish, but couldn't force herself to start on it.

"Did you have a good trip?" Ashleigh's fiancée questioned from the kitchen where he and Ashleigh were cooking dinner. Wynn pushed wisps of burnished brown hair from her eyes.

"It was nice to see my family. We have a baby cow," she added with a smile.

Ben chuckled at her change in subject. "What'd you name it? I know you did."

"How do you know?"

Ashleigh laughed. "You named your hairdryer. You give *every*thing a name."

Wynn did her best to look offended. She did have a habit of naming things, including inanimate objects. Her car was named Orville and her hairdryer was Windy.

"I named her Podie, if you must know."

"Podie. I like it," Ashleigh conceded.

"Taste this," she commanded Ben. He dutifully opened his mouth and she popped in a slice of tomato.

"Ughh," he said in disgust. Ashleigh nodded.

"I thought it looked bad, but I wasn't sure."

Wynn laughed at Ben's puckered lips. He quickly ran to the trashcan and spit out the bite.

"You tried to poison me," he accused.

"I'm sorry," she apologized, offering him a kiss as penance.

"So what did you two do today?" Wynn wondered, as she propped her feet up on the purple painted trunk they used as a coffee table.

"We went to the early service this morning. Then we went to Ben's parents' for lunch. Then Ben had a softball scrimmage."

"Who won?" Wynn inquired, though she already knew the answer. Faith Temple's softball team had not lost a game since Ben had joined the team.

"We did of course. The other team wasn't really a team. One of the guys told me they just get together to practice and goof off," Ben explained. "They were pretty good, though. The second baseman was really good."

Ashleigh pointed at Ben with the tip of her knife.

"Was that the one that looked so familiar?" she demanded. Ben pushed the blade away with his index finger.

"You really are trying to kill me.

"Yeah, 'that' was the one."

"I wish I could remember where I've seen him before. He had gorgeous eyes," she told Wynn. "Real blue. Like dish detergent."

Wynn began to laugh again. "Ashleigh, you amuse me."

"You've never told me I had gorgeous eyes," Ben pouted. Like a neglected child, he dragged his feet toward the refrigerator. He fetched the sour cream and taco sauce, all the while sulking like a two year old.

"You have gorgeous eyes, Ben. Real brown. Like a Hershey's bar. The kind with almonds."

Ben raised his eyebrows.

"I like the ones with almonds better than the regular

ones," she explained seriously. Wynn picked up a blue throw pillow and buried her face in it, laughing. Everyone loved Ashleigh. She made them laugh.

26

"I put the apples I bought in a basket in the fridge. They keep longer that way. I moved the dog food to the broom closet. It bothered me for it to be in the cabinet with your food. Make sure you eat that chocolate cake before it ruins. And you really shouldn't eat pizza for breakfast, Alex. It'll give you indigestion. I put all your underwear in the top drawer—"

"Mother!" She'd even rearranged his underwear drawer?

"Well, I was putting your laundry away. Everything was so unorganized. I know you're an adult now, but really Alex. You had boxers in with your t-shirts and socks with your jeans."

Alex shook his head in disbelief.

"I have to get to work," he told her. She nodded.

"Well, give me a kiss," Joan commanded him. He stooped to give her a peck on the cheek. She patted his shoulder.

"Thank you for letting me come this weekend. It was good to see you."

He reached for his thick jacket. "I'm glad you came, Mom. And not just because you washed my dishes and my laundry and did my grocery shopping." Busby brought a squeaky newspaper and laid it at his feet.

"Sorry, boy you have to stay outside today. I won't be home to let you out." The puppy whimpered.

"I can't believe my first grandchild has fur," Joan said with a sigh. Alex chuckled.

"Busby will be the only grandchild you're going to

have for a long while, Mom. Let me take him out back and then I'll carry your things out." He scooped up the squirming pup and the rubber paper and headed out the back door. The high, dog-eared fence blocked his view of the neighbors' yards. A weeping cherry tree grew in the corner of his twelve by fifteen foot yard. Busby's wooden doghouse sat under the tree. He made sure the gate was latched and allowed Busby to run free around the yard.

"Be good," he instructed, pointing a finger at the little, furry butterball. Busby yipped in acquiescence.

"One day you're going to figure out how to bark and our neighbors are going to shoot me." Busby gave another happy yip. Alex reached down and scratched the small head.

When he returned to the house, he found his mother on the phone.

"Oh, here he is now. I'll just let you talk to him. Nice speaking to you, too." She held the cordless phone out to her son.

"Who is it?" Alex wondered as he reached for it. She smiled brightly and covered the receiver.

"It's Pastor Polk. I put your phone number on the visitor's card I filled out."

Alex sighed and gave her a threatening look. She shrugged innocently. He snatched the phone away.

"Hello?"

"Hello, Dr. Chadwell, this is Leon Polk from Living Branch?"

"Hello. I was just heading out the door to work."

"Well, I was just calling you to invite you back to church and to tell you about our young adult Bible study on Wednesday nights. It's for young adults between the ages of eighteen and thirty. Starts at seven-thirty if you're interested."

Alex grimaced. "Sounds great. I'll think about coming," he lied.

"Great. Well it was good seeing you on Sunday. I hope you have a terrific day."

"Thanks. You, too." As he hung up, Joan stared at him in expectation.

"Nice man, isn't he?"

Alex waggled his finger at her. "Mother—"

"Well, I didn't tell him to call you. I just wrote down our names and your address and phone number. The bulletin said to."

"And do you always do what the bulletin says?" he questioned seriously. Joan stared at him for a moment and then began to laugh.

"You're going to make a good father."

Alex threw his hands up in frustration. "You're impossible."

27

The deli was crowded with students and business people on their lunch breaks. The warm ocher walls were covered with black and white photographs of Cincinnati. The menu was written on a blackboard with colored chalk. After ordering, Wynn shrugged out of her jean jacket and draped the garment across the back of the chair. An older woman already sat at the table, a basket of fries and a roast beef sandwich in front of her.

"Looks good. Maybe I should have ordered that," Wynn commented as she sat.

"It is good. I already snuck a bite. What did you get?" the woman inquired.

"Chicken salad croissant and sweet potato fries. I've been craving the fries since you suggested we come here.

"Bad news. I've only got forty-five minutes today. I have a meeting with my nursing instructor," she announced. The older woman rolled her gray eyes.

"Kids are so busy these days. Such a shame. Well if you've only got forty-five minutes, we've only got forty-five minutes. How was your week, Honey?"

"I had a good week. My brother and I went home to see my father on Saturday. I was all but promised a job at Children's which pleases me greatly. How was your week?"

"Oh pretty good. I went to the doctor on Thursday and was given a clean bill of health. Went down to the cemetery and visited Bill. It was a little nippy so I didn't stay long.

"I was wondering after you at church yesterday. Octavia told me you had gone home to Kentucky. I'd like to travel down there with you sometime."

"That would be fun. Oh, thank you," she smiled at the waiter who slid her meal in front of her.

"How about you pray?"

Wynn nodded and bowed her head. "Father, thank You for this day. Thank You for Clara and for her good health. Thank You for loving me on my good days and my bad. Please bless this food so that it might give nourishment to our bodies. In Christ's name."

"And please take all the calories and cholesterol out of this food so that I don't gain any more weight, Lord. Thanks," Clara added. "Amen."

Wynn laughed as she reached for a napkin and spread it across her lap.

"You're funny, Miss Clara."

Clara took a bite of her sandwich and shrugged her bony shoulders. Wynn had grown to love this little woman since they had been assigned to one another in the church's mentor program. Wynn had been wary when Ducky first tried to talk her into it. Wynn had felt she had enough people telling her what she needed to do, but Clara was truly a Godsend.

"Oh, I almost forgot to tell you. I found myself a man."

Wynn strangled on her iced tea. She sputtered and coughed while Clara reached to beat her on the back. Tears were streaming down her face and she was out of breath by the time she finally stopped coughing.

"Sorry. I suppose I should have waited for you to swalla first," Clara said, pursing her lips and surveying the younger woman. Wynn waved a napkin at her and coughed again.

"You found a man?" she choked out, picturing a cute, little, old guy with no teeth and a bow tie.

"Yes, I did. And my, my, he's the cutest thing I ever

saw in my life. Even handsomer than Bill used to be. He's tall. He's about a half a head taller than you and he has the brightest blue eyes and black curls. He has a dimple when he smiles."

"Sounds dreamy," Wynn laughed. She dipped a fry in sour cream and popped it in her mouth.

"Oh, he is, he is. There's one problem though."

"What's that?"

"I'm a few years older than he is," Clara admitted. Wynn shook her head.

"My Grandma Ivy was four years older than my Grandfather."

"Well I'm about forty-four years older than him."

Wynn burst into laughter. She was glad she was not in the process of swallowing this time. Clara looked pleased that Wynn found her so amusing. She waved off the waiter that came to see if they were in need of anything and waited for her young companion to sober.

"Oh, my sides hurt. So where did you find this man?" Wynn wanted to know.

"At church. He came with his mother yesterday. I was looking all around for you. I would have liked to introduce the two of you. I tell you Gwyneth honey, he was one of those men that there's a waiting list for. He's a little older than you I think. And I checked. No wedding ring."

"Clara Beetle, you're awful."

Clara shrugged. "Just keeping an eye out for my little girl. If I can find you a good man, it'll save you lots of trouble. Trust me, the looking around for one is the hard part." She winked and took another bite of her sandwich. Her eyes grew serious as she chewed.

"Well, honey, fifteen minutes gone and we haven't even

gotten to the important part. How're you?"

Wynn did not immediately answer. Things had been going well for months and then within the last few days things had turned topsy-turvy on her again. Her emotions were muddled once more.

"I feel like I'm on a rollercoaster sometimes. One minute everything is going wonderfully and the next I feel like I'm right back where I started from. I've grown so much. I've never been more assured of God's reality and His love for me, but ever so often I still feel angry with Him."

She poked her index finger at her croissant. "I miss Momma and Chassity, Caleb and Hope, but it's been so long. I don't think of them often. They aren't a part of my life anymore. Doesn't that sound so horrible?"

Clara covered her young hand with a wrinkled, bejeweled one. The soft skin and frail grip reminded Wynn that Clara was not as strong as she seemed. Not physically, anyway.

"God never meant for you to stop living. They're a part of you, but they're not present. I think that was the hardest part after I lost Bill. It's when I stopped aching for him that I grew most angry with God and myself. You feel as if you've betrayed them. But it's alright to let them go. In fact we're supposed to."

Wynn smiled wryly and fingered the checkered paper in her lunch basket.

"I wish my father could hear this."

"Ahh, is that why you're upset?"

She sighed. "It's been seven years, Miss Clara. He doesn't talk about them. He doesn't visit the graves. He doesn't go to church or pray over his meals. He hardly says two words except to talk about the animals. I can't understand why

God would do that to him after all he did for God."

"Oh, honey. God didn't do this to your father. Your father is doing this to himself. God's calling to him, reaching to him. He wants to heal all the hurt. Your father's just running," Clara said. Wynn looked into the wise, old eyes.

"Wouldn't it have been easier for God to have let Momma and my sisters and brother live and let Daddy go on preaching. Looks to me like that would have been in everyone's best interest."

"God didn't take your family, Gwyneth, but He welcomed them home. God'll use the bad things that happen if we only let Him. I know you've heard that everything happens for a reason. Probably heard it a million times. And it's true. God gives everything a reason—even the bad things. Every event impacts a million other things. Maybe God is using what happened to allow your brother to help others deal with their grief. Maybe you wouldn't be where you are if it hadn't happened. Maybe people you don't even know were impacted."

"But Daddy—"

"Is running from the good that could come of this. There's a verse that says the calling of God is irrevocable. God didn't tell your Daddy to stop preaching. Your Daddy did that all on his own.

"Just keep praying, honey. Even when the words are hard to say, even when you're angry, keep talking to God."

Wynn nodded and sighed. It was the same advice she had heard from dozens of others, but it was easier to hear it from a woman who had experienced and struggled with loss.

The two of them talked on for a bit longer before they ended their luncheon. After Wynn had walked Clara to her car, the elder lady turned her eyes to the flawless, October sky.

"Well, Lord. That little girl is going through the valley again. I know you know best, but seems like you could give her a little extra lovin' this week. I have a feeling, though, that she's in for a hard time. Stay with her, Lord. Let her turn to you, instead of turning from you."

28

"Patty told me you weren't feeling well. You look just fine to me," Alex said to his teen-aged patient. Lydale grinned from his bed.

"The nursing students were here."

Alex laughed. "That's horrible, man. She was really worried about you."

"So were the nursing students."

Alex shook his head with an amused smile. He had to admit that if he were in Lydale's position he would fake a stomachache, too.

"Well, looks to me like you'll be dismissed soon despite the sudden stomach virus."

Lydale grinned and leaned back into his pillows.

"I can't wait to get home. Mom said she'd make spaghetti and meatballs when I got home," Lydale confided. He reached for the fruit cup on the tray beside his bed.

"I'm tired of hospital food."

"I get to eat it everyday," Alex said with a grimace. "Well I have to get down to check on a few other patients, before I head to surgery."

"What do you get to do today?" Lydale wondered. There was interest in his dark eyes.

"I get to observe a heart surgery. Tomorrow I'm observing the removal of a tumor."

"That is so cool," Lydale said in admiration. Alex chuckled in spite of the seriousness of the upcoming surgeries.

"You're an interesting kid, Lydale. I'll see you around."

"See ya'," Lydale called, before turning his attention to

the PlayStation he'd had a nurse bring up for him. Alex left the room with an amused grin. He checked his watch. He had only a few minutes before he had to scrub in. He'd have to finish his checkups later. He started down the labyrinth of halls toward the O.R. Within minutes, he had his cap and mask on. He joined the others at the sink. Dr. Catrina Donovan scooted over to make room. Alex was amazed by her apparent calmness. This was her first surgery as lead surgeon.

"How're you today, Chadwell?" a masked man inquired. The man's eyes were mahogany and his forehead was tall and marked by years of concentration and concern.

"Good. How about you, Dr. Ramadas?" Alex asked, wiggling his nose in an attempt to reposition his mask.

"I'm very well, thanks," the doctor replied.

Alex nodded. He turned toward the operating room. There were three nurses and two nursing students waiting. Alex nodded a greeting to the nursing students, his fellow observers.

"Ladies and gentlemen, let's give this little boy a healthy heart," Dr. Donovan said before stepping up to the automatic, frosted glass sliding door. Alex fell into step behind the other doctors. The nursing students entered last of all and joined him in the corner where they would be out of the way. Thinking of Lydale, he glanced toward them. When he did, he met a pair of familiar green eyes. He couldn't place the pretty eyes with a name, but he was sure he had met this person before. His own eyes scrunched with a smile and the lady returned the greeting. Alex turned his attention to the small boy on the table. The anesthesiologist had finished with him. He seemed to be sleeping peacefully. Wires sprouted from the little body and linked him to a myriad of machines. Beside him lay a teddy bear with an identification bracelet wrapped around its neck like a necklace. A nurse picked up the stuffed animal and started to set it aside.

"May I hold it?" the green-eyed student questioned suddenly. The nurse's eyes creased with a soft smile.

"Sure." She relinquished the bear to the young woman. "His name is Jason."

Alex had once been told by an elderly doctor to never call the patient by name while in surgery. It made it more difficult. It added weight to the surgeon's shoulders. A name made the patient a real little boy or little girl.

Alex reached out and briefly touched the small hand lying on the table.

"Sleep well, Jason. When you wake up you're going to have a new heart."

He looked up to see a smile in Dr. Ramadas's eyes.

"Let's get started then, shall we?"

29

Wynn collapsed on her bed. The long day had exhausted her. She was the only one in the apartment. Ashleigh had left a note saying she was out with Ben. Ducky had a concert tonight. DeJanna and a few of the other girls had invited her to go to an Irish pub with them, but she had refused. She pulled her fuzzy, green blanket from the foot of the bed and wrapped it around her. She looked around the room she had lived in for the past two years. Her lavender walls were plastered with black and white posters of far away, European cities, places she hoped to visit someday.

Her mother's rocking chair sat in the corner by the seven-foot tall window. A quilt she and her mother had pieced together was thrown across the high back. Sheer curtains hung on copper rods above the window. Two mismatched bookcases were stacked on top of one another and held books and framed photographs. A tall chest of drawers stood between the bed and the wall. On top sat perfume bottles and another photograph. Her parents smiled at her from behind the glass. They stood with their arms around one another, while Wynn and her sisters sat on the soft, spring grass and held wriggling puppies. Gabe and Caleb knelt on either side of their sisters. The picture had been taken by a photographer parishioner at a church picnic just a few months before the accident. They had all been so happy that day. Wynn could look at the photograph now and smile. She could laugh at Caleb's cowlick and Hope's blue wind suit and orange socks. She reached over and fingered the wooden frame.

"God," she whispered, "help Daddy to move on. Help him to let go."

She paused staring at the photograph. "Let them know I love them. Let them know that I'm doing my best."

30

Alex sipped his coffee and skimmed the headlines. A hefty slice of chocolate cake sat on the stainless steel tabletop in front of him. The newspaper was full of bad news. Four more men killed in Iraq. A plane downed in Afghanistan. Four homicides in the tri-state area. It was enough to make a man sick. He dug through the paper and pulled out the comics.

"Well, look who it is. Why, I'm surprised you aren't here with some pretty, young lady."

Alex looked up, startled. His brow furrowed in confusion as a short, elderly woman in a peach flowered dress neared his table for two.

"Uh," he started, but the woman smiled a wide grin.

"Oh, I know you don't remember me. I'm Clara. Clara Beetle. From church?"

"Oh, yes. Hello. I'm sorry I didn't recognize you right away," Alex apologized as he stood. She waved him back into his seat and then took the one opposite him.

"Perfectly alright." She pointed a knotty finger toward a table of elderly women. "I'm here with a few of my girlfriends. I meet with them once a week. We're all widows. We come to scope out the men."

Alex was so surprised by this reply he choked on his laughter.

"So there I was, sitting and scoping and I looked over here and saw you all alone. I thought I would come over here and say hello and give a few old ladies something to gossip about," she announced nodding her head in the direction of her friends. Alex shook his head in amusement.

"So how are you, Mr. Chadwell?" Clara wanted to know.

"Please, it's Alex and I'm good, thanks. How are you?" Alex returned politely, still inwardly chuckling.

"Oh, I'm pretty good. God's given me a blessed week. It was real nice to have you in church on Sunday. I met with a friend on Monday and was telling her all about you. I hope to introduce the two of you on Sunday. She was visiting her family out of town last week."

Alex shifted in his seat. Clara Beetle was a very likable old woman. He almost hated to tell her he wouldn't be attending church on Sunday.

"Uh, I hadn't planned on being there on Sunday, Mrs. Beetle. You see I'm a doctor, a resident at Children's and well—"

"And you only came on Sunday to please your mother?" Clara reached out and patted his hand. "You don't need church, right? You're doing fine on your own?"

Alex lowered his brows and started to speak, but she interrupted again.

"I was the same way, you know. You see, I married when I was eighteen. Bill was so handsome and sweet. He was the sweetest man in the world, I do believe. We had five years together and then he was killed. His car stalled on the train track. He had been trying to beat it, probably. He was hurrying home to me and didn't want to wait on the train. I was pregnant with our first child. A boy." Her words were very matter of fact. She even smiled a little.

"When I got the news I collapsed. I lost Bill and the baby in one day. Before that we went to church. Bill was a Christian and I pretended I was one. After the accident, I didn't need God. I believed He existed but I figured I was better off without Him. And I did just fine on my own, too.

Bill left me a pension. I opened up a bookshop and I made a living for myself. I was doing fine."

Alex, interested in the woman's story despite himself, nodded.

"Then what happened?"

Clara shrugged and twisted the large ruby on her index finger.

"Nothing happened. That's just it. I just kept on grieving, missing Bill like crazy. I'd like to tell you that one day, God gave me a miracle and He healed the hurt and I came running back to Him. It wasn't like that. Nope. I started reading Bill's Bible and I read the Gospels. I saw what God had done for me, how He had given His Son to die and all. I felt obligated to accept Him. Sounds harsh and unchristian, I know. But that's how it was. I was so logical about the whole thing." She laughed at the memory and then looked at Alex.

"Since then God *has* healed the hurt and I have learned that He wants me to serve Him out of love and not obligation. It's been a long hard road, let me tell you. Sometimes I still get upset with God and sometimes I still find myself doing things for Him just out of obligation. Heaven knows what a hard time I had when I finally let go of Bill."

Clara reached out and patted his hand once more. "My point is God isn't just a crutch and He isn't something you turn to when life's not going well. Following Him is hard and takes strength, but completely worth it. Even when you're doing just fine." She smiled again and Alex wondered how this woman could have twisted the conversation around to the topic of religion. She was just like all the other Christians he'd met—preachy. Except this time, he was mildly interested.

"Well, listen to me. I didn't come over here to preach at you, Alex. I really didn't. I just never can help letting people know what God has done for me. I'll let you alone to enjoy your cake." She grinned broadly.

"I would like to see you back on Sunday, but you've got to make your own decision and I respect that. Well, it was good to see you. I'm going to head on back to my table and brag to my friends about you." She scooted off the seat. Alex stood.

"It was nice to see you again, Mrs. Beetle. I'll think about visiting your church again, but I won't make any promises," he told her. She smiled and reached a hand to pat his cheek.

"You're such a nice man."

She wandered back to her own table without another word. The elderly women with whom she was dining all turned appraising eyes in his direction. Alex sat back down, fighting a grin. He shook his head. This had been a strange meeting. If he didn't know better, he would think Someone was trying to tell him something. He glanced toward the skylights in the ceiling. Maybe, there was more to this God-thing than he had thought.

31

Wynn lifted her literature book from the passenger seat and pulled her keys from the ignition. She had rushed home from church to change into a heavy sweater and a pair of jeans and grab her book and a peanut butter sandwich. She climbed out of the car and jogged over the parking lot, down the hill, and toward the baseball diamond. The game had already started, but by the look of the scoreboard, no one had scored a run yet. She smiled at some of the women on the sidelines and picked her way over to where Ashleigh had an empty lawn chair waiting for her.

"You made it," Ashleigh beamed. Wynn settled into the plastic chair, accepting the can of pop that Ashleigh offered.

"Yes, I did. I promised your fiancée that I would come to one of his games and here I am." She popped the top of her soda and studied the field. The opposing team was up to bat.

"How much have I missed?"

"It's the second half of the first inning. Ben made it to second before the third out. What did you bring to read?"

Wynn held up her book. "British Literature. I am writing a paper on Jane Austin and her portrayal of women."

Ashleigh wrinkled her nose. She hated writing papers. "Sounds like loads of fun."

"I didn't figure I'd get anything read, but I thought I'd keep up the pretense that I'm a good college student and carry the book around. Who's that batting?"

Ashleigh squinted and studied the man standing at the plate, flicking the bat in anticipation.

"I can't remember what Ben said his name was. Potter

or Patterson. Porter. I think his last name was Porter. See the guy there? The one leaning on the fence. He's the one with the dish detergent eyes." She pointed to a tall figure dressed in baseball stirrups and a t-shirt from Joe's Crab Shack. A baseball hat and dark sunglasses effectively hid his face.

"I wish he'd turn around so you could see him.

"So how was church this morning?"

"Pastor Leon preached the second half of a sermon on Joseph. It was really very interesting. And Ducky sang a solo this morning. It was a gorgeous song. I want a copy of the lyrics. How was your service?" Wynn inquired, flipping open her book in vain. The Porter guy hit the ball into left field and just made it to first base.

"Reverend Lee preached on the Fruit of the Spirit. He made me hungry for kiwifruit."

Wynn laughed. "You are so funny, Ashleigh."

"I wasn't meaning to be. There he is. He turned. Does he look familiar to you?" she demanded, pointing excitedly toward the man on the other team.

"I can't see him very well. He's too far away," she said with a shrug. She watched as a bulky man hit a foul ball.

"I am going to have to have Ben introduce the two of you after the game."

"Mmm. Probably can't. I have to be at the hospital at four."

"Orientation on a weekend?" Ashleigh questioned. Wynn beamed.

"Yup. I have six hours on the floor tonight. I'm already scheduled for next Sunday. Corey, the guy who does the scheduling at the nursing home, worked it out so that I don't have to finish out the full two weeks."

"Very cool. But the game will be over way before four. See. That's the third out. First inning's already over."

Wynn didn't want to be introduced to the softball player but she didn't say so. Ashleigh was unstoppable once she had something in her head. She'd just leave a few minutes before the game ended and avoid the unwanted introduction.

Wynn's plans were thwarted. The game was so close she couldn't force herself to leave. By the last inning the teams were tied. The fans were on their feet, holding their breath. Wynn had long forgotten her literature book. Ben's team was on the field. The other team had a man on first, two outs, and two strikes. Ben was pitching and a spindly, tattooed man was at the plate. The Pirates had never lost a game and Ben was pitching his hardest. The blue-eyed guy was on first and inching his way toward second. Wynn had played softball in high school and now found it harder to watch than it had been to play. Her hands were clasped in front of her mouth. Ben threw a fastball. The bat cracked. The ball soared through the air and the men began running. Wilson Spalding ran for the ball but he just missed it. It hit the ground and bounced. He scooped it up and threw it toward third. By the time the ball hit the third baseman's glove, the other team's second baseman was nearing home. Marquis Gordon threw the softball toward home. The runner dove into a slide. The ball smacked into the pitcher's mitt just as his fingertips touched home. The umpire, a short, energetic tenor from Faith Temple's choir, shouted "Safe!"

Ben hung his head as the other team ran onto the field. The runner stood up and grinned as he dusted himself off.

"Poor Ben," Ashleigh sympathized. She grabbed

Wynn's arm and dragged her toward the field as Ben jogged in to home base. He congratulated the man, slapping him on the back. He suddenly stopped grinning and looked at the man's bare forearm.

"Ashleigh, run and get the first aid kit from my truck. Wynn, I have a patient for you," he yelled out as the two women neared. Ashleigh nodded and started off at a run. The crowd of men and their families parted as Wynn drew closer. Ben pointed to the man's arm.

"He slid hard. Wynn's a nurse. Well almost," he explained to the man. The man shrugged as he removed his sunglasses.

"It's nothing. Just a little sand burn," he objected. Wynn studied the bleeding arm. The skin had been scraped away and sand and pebbles were lodged in the raw, pink skin. His elbow was torn. The slide had burned the skin that wasn't ripped and dust coated the entire wound.

"Nice slide," she commented. He grinned.

"Thanks."

Ashleigh was right. He did have nice eyes. And he did look very familiar. Someone brought over a lawn chair and the Porter guy pushed him into it.

"Really. I can take care of this. I'm a doc—" he started to protest again. Porter slapped him on the back of the head.

"Shut up, man, and let the lady do her job," he commanded with a wink. Wynn's cheeks warmed and she wanted to stomp on Porter's toe. A tall, husky man stepped forward and handed her an unopened bottle of water and a sports towel.

"You're a doctor?" she asked. He nodded.

"Well, Ben, I can't give care if the patient refuses it," she announced lightly with a shrug.

"He's not refusing care, are you, Doc?" Porter demanded, slapping him on the head again. The injured man stared at him in disbelief.

"Are ya?" Porter reached to slap him again, but the man punched him in the stomach.

"I'm not refusing care, but I don't need an audience," he said pointedly, staring down his teammates. They got the hint and the entire group started off the field with shouts of "Good game!" and "We'll get you next time!"

The man grinned sheepishly, pushed up his short arm sleeve, and held his arm out to Wynn. She twisted the lid off the bottle as Ashleigh ran up with the first aid pouch.

"Could you hand me a pair of gloves," she asked her friend. Ashleigh unzipped the kit and dug around for a pair of latex gloves.

"So you're a doctor?" Ben questioned while Wynn pulled on her gloves. She poured water over his arm and gently wiped away the sand and dust. She felt the muscles in his arm tense under her fingers. The water was cold and she was sure the rough towel hurt his raw skin.

"Yeah. Hopefully someday a pediatric surgeon."

Wynn looked up in surprise. "Really? I'm going to be a pediatric nurse. I'm in my last year at UC."

His eyes squinted. "I thought I recognized your eyes. Were you observing a heart surgery at Children's this week?"

"Yes! You were the resident observing, weren't you?" she demanded. A smile slid across his face and he nodded. She reached for the opened pouch Ashleigh held out to her and found an alcohol pad.

"I hate this part," the doctor grumbled as she ripped open the package.

"It will only hurt a little bit," she chided.

"They teach you to say that, but it's not true," he said knowingly. Wynn smiled.

"You just tore your arm open and didn't flinch. You can handle a little alcohol pad." She cleaned the wound, pressing as carefully as she could. He sucked in air through his teeth, making a whistling noise. She tossed the pad to the ground.

"Could you hand me some antibiotic ointment and some gauze pads?"

Ashleigh complied and placed the packaged cream in her hand. She rubbed the ointment over the scraped skin and laid the gauze on top. She reached for a rolled bandage and wrapped his arm past his elbow, taping off the end with medical tape.

"There, good as new," she said, picking up the garbage and removing her gloves around the trash.

"Was I a good patient? Do I get a Snoopy Band-Aid?" he inquired. She checked her jean pockets. She always carried character bandages in her scrubs, but unfortunately she didn't stock her jean pockets. She smiled and shook her head.

"Sorry. I don't have any with me."

"And I don't usually keep Snoopy Band-Aids in my first aid kit," Ben supplied. The doctor shrugged.

"I'll just get one when I get to work. And a lollypop, too. A grape one."

Wynn wrinkled her nose. "Eww, grape?"

"Yeah. They're the best," he announced, hopping up from the chair and folding it.

"Nope, the lime ones are the best," Ben contradicted. Ashleigh shook her head.

"The cherry ones are," she disagreed as she zipped up the pouch.

"Green apple," Wynn corrected. All three of the others looked disgusted and she laughed at their expressions.

"Y'all just don't have as refined tastes as I do." She glanced down at her watch. It was a quarter past three.

"I have to go," she announced.

"It was nice to meet you. Thanks for fixing my arm," the doctor said, patting his mummified appendage.

"No problem. I'm Wynn Redecke, by the way."

32

Alex felt the blood drain from his face. He stumbled over nothing. His mouth felt like powder.

"Gwyneth Redecke?" he asked in a whisper. Wynn's pretty smile started to droop.

"Yes. How did you know?"

Alex felt his stomach drop to his feet and the world began to tilt. He turned his face from her as images of the car and the rain and Hope flooded to his mind.

"Oh, God," he murmured. How could he not have immediately recognized her? She had grown up, become a lady, but those eyes were the same. Hadn't he seen those eyes in all his nightmares?

"Are you alright?" she questioned. She touched his arm. He forced himself to look at her. His breath caught in his throat. Her face was masked with concern.

"Wynn," he began. He paused and took a breath. "I'm Alex, Alexander, Chadwell."

Recognition was immediate. Wynn's face paled and Ashleigh gasped. Wynn could only stare at him, blinking in disbelief. She was shocked. Her mouth parted as if she were going to say something, but instead she turned and walked away. Ashleigh ran after her. Ben stood in confusion.

"Hey Lee, Chadwell, are you coming?" Steve Perch called as he approached. "Alex, Melissa and I want you to come over and have dinner with us. What's wrong?"

Ben nodded. "Yeah. What just happened?"

Alex rubbed a hand over his face. The vivid memories played over in his mind. He had spent years mixing therapy and alcohol trying to be rid of them, but now they were back. The remembered sound of the rain falling through the treetops, splashing against the twisted metal, sizzling on the hot engine burned his ears. He could hear her crying. He felt her hand, sticky with blood and cold, so cold.

"Alex?"

Alex's head shot up. Steve and Ben were staring at him.

"What's wrong, man?"

Alex took a few deep breaths. He covered his face with his hands.

"I think you need to sit down, buddy," Steve said, pointing him toward the bench.

"How do you know, Wynn?" Ben demanded once he was seated.

"Wynn lost her family in an accident."

Ben nodded, apparently aware of the fact. Steve waited for him to continue.

"I was driving the truck that sent them into the ravine."

33

Wynn refused to speak to Ashleigh. She shut the door and started the engine. She felt only shock at the revelation. She backed out of the parking lot with Ashleigh helplessly staring after her, and calmly drove across town to the hospital. Thoughts and memories flurried in her mind.

He was Alexander Chadwell. He was the boy from high school. The football player and baseball star. He was the broken, young man that had shown up at the cemetery. The boy who had come to assuage his guilt, but had inflicted her family with more pain. He was the driver, the one that survived. He was a doctor? A pediatric doctor at her hospital. He had done well for himself it would seem. He probably never even thought of her family. She shook her head in disgust.

She parked her car in the parking garage and the reality of it all hit her. She hated Alexander Chadwell. Hated him for walking away from that crash. Angry tears swelled in her eyes.

She was supposed to report to the charge nurse in less than ten minutes, but she didn't have the strength to move from her car.

"God, I don't understand this," she whispered. "Just as everything was starting to be normal. How could you do this? How could you let him be here? God, this isn't fair. I've been trying so hard. I've been trying so hard to stop hating, to end the anger."

The tears wet her cheeks and she wiped her nose on the back of her hand. Alexander Chadwell being there changed everything and nothing all at once. When she believed him to be far away, it had been easy to not think of him. Even, occasionally, pity him. In truth, she had not given much thought to him in the past few years except to wish that his vehicle had been the one slammed into the ravine. Now he was here and living a full, successful life.

Wynn had tried to forgive him. The police had said the accident had not been his fault. A limb had fallen in the road and neither he nor her mother had had enough time to react. But Wynn had needed someone to hold responsible. When she no longer blamed God, Alexander Chadwell had become the recipient of her blame.

She glanced at her watch. She had to report in. She needed this job, wanted this job, but she felt sick. How could she work at the same place as *him*? She would have to refuse the job. She could work at another hospital. Most had pediatric floors. She could go back to Kentucky after graduation. There was a children's hospital in Lexington and one in Louisville. She wiped her eyes.

"God, I've wanted to work here for years. Why do I have to give it up? Why did you have to let him work here?" she demanded. She sighed and flung open her door. With one foot on the pavement, she paused.

"I won't let him ruin things again," she declared. "I won't let Alexander Chadwell ruin my plans."

Wynn gathered her bag. She would not let him do this again. Angry and distracted she entered the building, changed, and reported to the charge nurse.

34

Alex ran a hand through his thick curls. Every muscle in his body felt tense. How could this have happened? How could they both have moved here, attended the same school, work at the same hospital? If there was a God, why would He let this happen? Why were their lives being shattered all over again? After all he had been through? He had finally begun to forget, to move on. He was doing fine.

"Alex, are you going to be alright?" Steve questioned from the other side of Alex's Jeep Liberty. The others had left. Ashleigh had gone straight to Ben's truck once Wynn had pulled away. Ben had been at a loss. He hadn't known what to say. And what could he say? Nothing. He had turned and walked up the hill.

Alex had been standing at his Jeep now for ten minutes, just staring at its shining, maroon exterior. He had never expected to see Gwyneth Redecke again in his life. Her father had taken her and her brother far enough away that they were never supposed to cross paths again. Alex had been glad when they moved away. He had been gladder still when he had graduated and left behind the whisperings behind his back and the stares he'd received. He had moved to Cincinnati the week after he graduated.

He turned toward Steve.

"Is this your God's sense of humor? Does He think this is funny?" he demanded, his eyes flashing. A surprised look lifted Steve's dark brows.

"Why did He send her here? Do you know how hard this has been to get over?"

"Yeah. I was the one that drove you home every time

you got drunk trying to forget about it," Steve reminded. Alex raked his fingers through his hair again. He had given up the alcohol two years ago, but before that it had been his greatest reprieve. Much more effective than the therapists. He had never told his friends about the accident. They had never questioned his need to escape reality. They had happily joined him, drowning the stresses and difficulties of their lives. Everyone except Steve.

"Do you know how it must have looked to her? It looked like I didn't even care. I killed four people and I'm playing softball. I'm a doctor! Three children and a mother dead and I'm going to be a pediatric surgeon!"

"Alex—"

"Do you know how often I've thought about her? She has a twin brother and a father. Her father told me he would never forgive me. Never forgive me, Steve. You know why? Because I didn't die." He looked at his hand.

"I saw them. She was so small. Four or five. The blood was everywhere. She asked me if I was an angel." He swallowed hard. Steve's eyes were growing moist.

"She asked me to hold her hand. I was holding her hand when she died. And I've spent years trying to forget about her."

Steve said nothing as he waited for him to continue. Alex rubbed a hand over his bandaged arm.

"Why would He do this? Am I being punished?"

Steve scratched his scruffy chin and blinked quickly to dry his eyes.

"Maybe the Lord has greater plans than you could understand. He wouldn't bring the hurt back without wanting to heal it. I think you convinced yourself that you were doing well enough on your own, but in truth you've never gotten over this, Alex. You've been running away from it and trying to bury it, but it's always been there. The struggle was obvious.

"Man, I've been praying for you for years and this is the first time I've ever heard you acknowledge God. Maybe the time has come to really move on, let it go, let them go."

"Why her? Why Gwyneth?" Alex demanded. Steve shrugged.

"I don't have the answers, Alex," he replied gently.

"Then who does?"

35

The sky was never dark over Cincinnati. All the lights lit the night sky, turning it a pale pink-gray. Stars never shined over the city. She missed the stars. Wynn parked her car in a visitor space. She shivered as she left the warmth of the vehicle. The evening had not gone well. She had been distracted and emotional all evening. One of the other care techs had been gruff with her. She would do better next time, she promised herself.

She waited at the corner for the light to turn. She ran across the street, dodging a group of rowdy students. Gabe was waiting for her at the door.

"Wynn, what's wrong?" he demanded, swinging open the door and stepping to the side so that she could enter the dormitory. She huddled in her jacket, willing the chill to leave her body.

"Can we go to your room?" she questioned, glancing around at the busy lobby. He led her toward the elevators and did not push her to talk. She had called him just after she had clocked out. She had not been able keep the distress from her voice and he had immediately picked up on it.

A few people greeted them as they started down Gabe's hall. There was a party at the end of the hall and students with Styrofoam cups spilled into the hallway.

Gabriel sighed and pointed to his door. "Go on in. I have to go check this out."

Wynn nodded and slipped inside his room. He had been writing a paper. The radio was playing and the computer curser blinked at the end of a half-finished sentence. The room was a mess. Clothes were in a pile beside the empty hamper. His garbage can overflowed with crumpled papers and TV dinner boxes. Books were stacked on the lumpy futon and his bed had not been made. There were magazines and copies of the school paper strewn across the floor.

Wynn pushed the books to the side and settled on the uncomfortable futon. She noticed Gabe's Bible lying open on the top of the stack. A Scripture was highlighted with blue ink. She scanned the words and snorted. She glanced toward the ceiling. Of course, it would be opened to such a Scripture.

"So that on the contrary, you ought rather to forgive and comfort him, lest perhaps such a one be swallowed up with too much sorrow. Therefore I urge you to reaffirm your love to him" (2 Corinthians 2:7 and 8).

The door was flung open and Gabriel entered.

"They're okay," he said, referring to the partiers down the hall. He glanced at his sister.

"I've started a new Bible study. On forgiveness," he announced, as he bent to survey the contents of his small fridge.

"Have you had supper? I have some corndogs I can run down the hall and pop in the microwave," he offered. Wynn shook her head.

"Why forgiveness?"

Gabe shrugged. "I don't know. It just felt relevant. Here, I know you haven't eaten. Eat this and tell me what's wrong." He tossed a foil wrapped cheeseburger at her. She caught it.

"How old is this?" she inquired with a raised brow.

"You don't want to know."

She shrugged, unwrapped the cold leftover, and took a bite. The bread was soggy and mayonnaise oozed out the side.

"What is this verse talking about." She pointed at the opened page. Gabe took a bite of a frozen corndog and craned his neck to look at the Scripture. His nose wrinkled.

"These aren't good frozen. It's talking about a church member who committed a sin and paid the price of it. Paul was telling the church members to forgive him and accept him back with love. If they didn't the man would be eaten up with his sorrow and God doesn't want that. He wants us to forgive and be forgiven. He doesn't want us to live in continual grief and guilt." He laid his corndog on his TV stand and reached for a bag of cheese curls and a paperback book lying nearby.

"Here let me read it to you from *The Message* translation because I like the way it says it. 'Now is the time to forgive this man and help him back on his feet. If all you do is pour on the guilt, you could very well drown him in it. My counsel now is to pour on the love'. Isn't that awesome?" Gabe asked, always excited and enthusiastic about his study of the Scriptures.

Wynn sighed. She knew that God was showing her something. She did not believe in coincidence. The events of the past weeks were connected and purposeful. First, the lapse in her progress, the reminders of the accident, the hurt of her father's transformation. And now, Alex Chadwell had magically appeared after seven years and God was handing her verses about forgiveness.

"I met Alex Chadwell today," she told her brother quietly. When he didn't say anything, she looked up to find him staring at her blankly.

"Who?" he finally asked. Wynn looked at him in disbelief.

"Alexander Chadwell? You don't remember him?"

"The name sounds familiar."

Wynn could not believe that Gabe could ever forget that name. How could he?

"Gabe, he was the one that killed them."

Recognition washed his features. He sat comprehending the information for a long moment. He set his cheese curls to the side.

"Wynn, he didn't kill them," he finally said. Wynn sat still, shocked by Gabriel's reaction to the news.

"He was driving the other car. He—"

Gabe sighed, sorry that he was upsetting his sister more with words he felt he had to say.

"He was driving to school in the rain. Momma stopped because of the tree branch. He swerved to miss her. Wynn, he didn't kill them." He moved to sit beside her, pushing books and papers onto the floor with a thud.

"He's been the easiest one to blame. Him and God. I blamed them both for a while. Then I blamed myself. And I blamed Momma for driving on that road in the rain. I blamed Chassity and Caleb for having to be driven to school. I blamed Dad for not keeping Hope with him." He paused and squeezed her shoulder.

"It doesn't work, Wynn. It doesn't make things better. It doesn't make things easier. It doesn't bring them back. None of us are to blame. Not me, not you, not Alex, not God."

Wynn stared at her hands. She had felt all those things, had blamed them all, had experienced all the pain Gabriel had. How had he let it all go? Why did it continually tear at her? Why couldn't she overcome it all as Gabe had?

"You're letting what happened consume you. The past is affecting every part of your future. Don't let it, Wynn,"

Gabe advised. She made a face at him. She had always hated when he told her what to do. He grinned.

"You always look so lovely when you make that face," he said sarcastically. He tugged her ponytail.

"You sound like an old sage."

"Thanks." Gabe stood and snatched his cheese curls back up.

"So what does he do now? Manager at a car wash?"

Wynn held out a hand to ask for part of his snack. He dumped some into her hand.

"He's a pediatric doctor at Children's," she told him, trying to keep the bitterness from her voice. She could see the wisdom in her brother's words, but words alone did not make the hurtful feelings go away. Gabe turned to stare at her.

"Oh. Wynn, I'm sorry. What are you going to do?"

Wynn shrugged. "I'm not going to let him make me lose this job. It's a big hospital. We'll never see one another. I know, Gabe. I'm supposed to be a saint like you and forgive and forget, but it won't be that easy for me. I'll make do, though. I have enough people praying to make up for my lack of faith."

"I'm not a saint and if I had met him on the street you would have had to been the one telling me all these things," Gabe confessed. He reached out and fingered the frame housing a family picture. Wynn stood and scoured the refrigerator for a pop.

"I wouldn't have told you those things."

"I think I would actually like to meet him."

Wynn straightened, banging her knuckles on the refrigerator shelf. "What?"

"I need to let him know I forgive him. Like the verse

says. I can only imagine how this has affected him."

Wynn stared at him. He couldn't be serious.

"Affected? He didn't look *affected* to me. He's a rich, good looking, surgeon who plays softball on Sunday afternoons," Wynn scoffed, popping the tab on her can vengeance. Gabe shrugged.

"I'd bet you a million bucks he's suffered depression, probably chronic depression and has turned to substances or other things to gain relief."

"Oh, stop being a psychologist for once, and be a normal human. Besides you don't gamble and you don't have a million dollars. If you had seen the man I saw today you wouldn't be so eager to make your diagnoses."

Gabe shrugged again. Muffled trilling startled Wynn and she jumped, stumbling over a smelly basketball shoe.

"That's the phone," he clarified. He surveyed the room. "Question is, where is it?"

Gabe started throwing clothes and papers and magazines around the room as he searched for the cordless phone. Wynn turned over an empty popcorn bag. The phone lay underneath, the ID screen blinking blue. Her brother snatched it up.

"Redecke."

A slow smile covered his face and he leaned against the desk. Wynn guessed from his sudden look of pleasure that Ducky was on the other end.

"Yeah, she's here. She's alright."

"I figured Ashleigh had related the whole story." He rolled his eyes at his sister. She smiled a little. Yes, Ashleigh had probably told the story to everyone to whom they were mutually acquainted. She popped a cheese curl in her mouth and chomped.

"I thought I might drive her home. Would you be willing to drive her back in the morning to get her car? What time do you have class?" he asked of Wynn.

"Ten."

"Ten," he repeated. Ducky must have objected. "I'll treat you to breakfast. I have some Space Marshmallow cereal somewhere in my closet. The milk expired only three days ago."

Wynn laughed. Her brother needed to get married right out of college or he would die of malnutrition or food poisoning.

"I would offer to take you to dinner, but I'm a poor college student. I could probably swing bologna sandwiches and some pork rinds. Come on, it's an all-American meal. You could invite me to eat over there a little more often since my darling sister isn't going to."

Wynn settled back onto the couch and listened to Gabe's side of the banter.

"Just ask her out, already. I'll loan you the money," Wynn offered. The change in subject was welcomed. She was tired of thinking about Alex Chadwell and forgiveness. Better to dwell on her brother's serious need of her expert matchmaking skills than on the detestable Dr. Chadwell.

Gabe didn't bother to cover the receiver.

"She'd never say yes. What? Oh." He glanced at Wynn once more. "She said yes."

"See and you didn't even have to ask her."

36

Alex had not slept well the night before. When he did finally drift off, he had a nightmare and jerked awake. He had spent from two o'clock in the morning until five watching a Three Stooges marathon. It had made him laugh a little.

He had tried not to think about her. He had tried not to think about God and whatever role He had played in the past few weeks. Steve was right. He had never before believed that God existed. Now he was ready to concede. Coincidence couldn't be intentional. Fate would never know how to punish him so thoroughly. There had to be a God.

He ran a hand over his eyes. He was finishing the thirteenth hour of what was supposed to have been a twelve-hour shift. His body was incredibly tired. His eyes were heavy and his responses were seconds slower than usual. He needed to focus. He needed to stop letting his mind wander. The accident and Gwyneth Redecke and God would have to wait. He had a patient to check up on—a young girl who'd recently had intestinal surgery. She was eight years old, but her body was small for her age. She had a beautiful smile. She was missing a tooth in the front. He entered her room and found a small crowd of people and a menagerie of stuffed animals waiting there.

"Hello," he greeted the gathered family and the skeletal, little girl lying on the bed. "I'd like to do a little check up on Anna." All of the guests but the parents scooted out the door.

"Hi, Anna. Do you remember me?" he asked of the

droopy-eyed eight-year-old. She gave him a tired smile.

"Dr. Alex?"

"Yup. How're you feeling?" he asked, opening the folder and pulling a pen from his lab coat.

"Sleepy," she murmured. He checked her IV and the vitals a nurse had scribbled down earlier. Alex half-faked a yawn.

"Yeah, me too," he informed her, smiling when her small mouth opened wide, catching the yawn contagion. She was on morphine for the pain. Her brown eyes were hazy and she seemed a little groggy.

"Does your tummy hurt any?" he inquired. She took a moment to respond.

"Um-hmm, a little."

"Anything else hurt?"

Anna stared at the wall a moment and finally shook her head. Her mother, who stood clutching the rail of Anna's bed, spoke.

"She said her head hurt earlier," she supplied. Her husband nodded to confirm the complaint. Alex made a note of that.

"We'll see what we can do about that. I need to have a look at the incision," he announced, folding back blankets.

"Looks like you have a lot of friends here," Alex said, nodding toward all the stuffed animals. Anna smiled. He checked the incision. The stitches were neat and small. The skin around was red and bruised. The wound was healing as it should. Alex raised the covers and smiled at her parents.

"She's doing just fine. You're pretty good at this healing thing, Anna. A couple days and you'll be home again. I can't believe you're trying to leave me so soon."

He looked to the worried parents. "I'll tell the nurse

about the headache and what to give her for it. If she complains anymore about it, let the nurse know. I'll run by for another visit tomorrow. I hope you all have a good night." He pointed to stuffed dog with his pen. "That one looks like my dog."

"Name?" Anna asked, drowsily.

"Of my dog?"

She nodded.

"Busby."

"I'll name 'im Busby then," she told him, letting her eyelids drop. He smiled.

"Busby'd be honored. I'll see you tomorrow, Miss Anna." He nodded to the parents and exited the room. The three people who had quit the room earlier were lined against the walls awaiting reentry.

"You can go back in now." They thanked him and cleared the hallway. Alex made a stop at the nurse's station and completed his round. Finally, he gathered his things from his locker and said goodnight to the people gathered in the lounge. He was ready to go home, feed Busby, and fall into bed. He would sleep well tonight. He might take a few sleeping pills just to be sure.

37

"Dr. Chadwell?"

Alex turned to see a tall man standing behind him. Alex felt a knot in his stomach. Would there never be an end to this? Gabriel Redecke knew that he was recognized and did not bother to introduce himself.

"I'd like to talk to you for a few moments, if you have the time."

Alex nodded. Better to let Redecke rail at him and get it over with. He pointed down a long hallway.

"Will the cafeteria suit?"

"Cafeteria's fine."

Alex rubbed the back of his neck and started down the hall toward the elevators. The younger man followed silently behind. Alex could only imagine what he had come for. Was he also a student at UC? Or had he come all the way from Kentucky to confront him? Alex pushed the button and waited for the elevator.

"I suppose your sister told you about our meeting, yesterday?" He knew it was a stupid question, but he felt the need to say something.

"She was surprised to see you. She's spent the last seven years either forgetting about you or hating you," Gabriel replied, stepping onto the empty elevator.

"Oh."

A man and a woman stepped onto the elevator putting a hold on the men's conversation. The two of them remained silent as they traversed the concourse and passed the gift shop and convenience store. When they reached the cafeteria, Alex poured himself a large coffee.

He watched the man fill a forty-two ounce cup with Mountain Dew. "Thirsty?" he asked Gabriel.

"A little."

Alex paid for both beverages. Gabriel pointed out a small table in a corner. The surrounding tables were empty. Alex nodded and sat, loosening the top button of his dress shirt.

"Alright," he said with a sigh. He motioned for Gabriel to begin.

"You're probably wondering why I'm here."

"I had never expected to see you or your sister again. I've already been told I would never be forgiven so there was really no point in looking you up."

Gabriel rested his forearms on the table and interlocked his fingers.

"Wynn's very upset. She had pictured you being a bit more affected by the accident. She never expected you to be a successful doctor. It kills her that you're working in the same place she is. It's been hard for her." Alex looked away, but Gabriel continued.

"She went through three years of depression. She gave up on her faith, blamed herself, hated everyone. She started coming back when she moved here and started attending church again. It's still hard for her."

Alex said nothing. Gabriel shrugged.

"It's been even worse for Dad. Mom was his everything and he loved my sisters and brother more than his own life. He would have died for them." Gabriel stared at the table, seeming to see things that weren't there. It was a long moment before he looked up again.

"Now he's turned away from everything he was. He can't understand why God would take away what meant so much to him. He doesn't talk about them anymore. He's put all the pictures away and he never mentions their names or God, for that matter. He runs a farm. He's slowly killing himself working from sunup to sundown, seven days a week."

Alex swallowed hard. The man knew just where to hit. He knew that yelling and anger would have had less affect. Hearing all of this hurt worse.

"And me? Everybody says I handled it the best. One suicide attempt, two years of counseling, and I'm told I've adjusted. I'm a Psychology major at Xavier." He fell silent for a moment. When Alex looked at him there was a hardness in his eyes that bespoke of years of anger.

"She wasn't lying. It brings things back. Seeing you makes the grief resurface," he said. Alex held his hands up in surrender.

"I didn't mean for this to happen. I didn't mean to mess things up for her or for you. God knows, the last thing I want to do is bring you all more pain. I've regretted that day. I wish I had died instead. I wish I had never woke up that morning. God knows how many times I've wished that."

"You're not going to tell me how the accident ruined *your* life?" Gabriel asked, his dark brows raised. Alex leaned back in the booth and studied the man.

"The accident didn't ruin my life. I almost did. I thought about suicide, but decided it would be the easy way out. I started drinking and found that worked, but it was just a slower form of suicide. I tried to forget you all, too. All of you. Hope was the hardest to forget." He paused.

"But I was doing well. Real well. And then my mom came to visit and she convinced me to go to church with her.

For the first time I started to seriously consider that there might be a God, and then I met your sister again. These past few weeks have been insane. Things keep happening that could never happen on their own. There have been too many interrelated events. And now here you are. Why?"

Gabriel studied his hands. He seemed to be searching for words.

"After Wynn finished work yesterday she came to see me. We're twins, you know, and there is some truth to that whole twin connection thing. We've always been close. We've always gone to one another when something was bothering us. Well, last night you were bothering her. I had just finished my Bible study when she came and I had read this verse." He pulled a piece of paper from the pocket of his jacket. He laid it on the tabletop and slid it toward Alex.

Alex accepted the slip of paper and read the sprawling script.

"Now is the time to forgive this man and help him back on his feet. If all you do is pour on the guilt, you could very well drown him in it. My counsel now is to pour on the love. 2 Corinthians 2:7 and 8."

"It's from the Bible. Paul was talking about a man, a Christian, church member, who had sinned and been chastised for it. He was saying that this man should be forgiven and accepted or the sorrow, the grief and guilt, would destroy him. Paul was telling the church to tell him that they forgave him and that they cared about him despite his sin."

Alex lowered his brows, confused.

"A psychologist would say you have to let go of the past, but I think the past needs to let go of you first. So, here it is. I forgive you for being in that accident. I forgive you for walking away when my mother and sisters and brother died. I thank you for calling 911 and for trying to save them. I even respect you for coming to the cemetery that day. I can't say that it's easy for me to do this or that I'm glad that you're doing so well. There's a part of me that still wishes that the outcome had been reversed. I have hated you just because God allowed you to live and my family to die. And for that I ask your forgiveness."

Alex could only stare at Gabriel Redecke. He had not been expecting this. He had readied himself for anger and accusations.

"I don't understand."

Gabriel smiled slightly and shrugged.

"You said you were just beginning to think there might be a God. Well, I wholeheartedly believe there is one and He doesn't want you to live life haunted by something that happened seven years ago. He wants to heal you of all the hurt, just as He has done me, and as He is healing Wynn."

Alex leaned back in his chair, stunned by the man's words, by the correlation of the past weeks' events. There had to be a God. A very relentless God. What did He mean by all of this? What was He trying to do?

"You look a little thrown. You okay?" Gabriel wondered. Alex shook his head.

"No." He looked up; his face was tired and confused.

"What does God want from me?"

This time Gabriel looked surprised as if the question had caught him off guard.

"He's making me confront what I've buried, what I thought I had moved past. And why now? Why is He trying to get at me now? My mom's been a Christian for years and one of my college buddies has been touting Christ since I've known him. You and Wynn are what? Seniors? We've been living in the same town for four years. I'm a UC graduate. Why am I just now running into you? Why is this happening now?"

Gabriel shrugged. "Maybe it's not just happening now. Maybe God has been pursuing you all this time and you're just now ready to listen."

Alex sighed and rubbed his hand over his tired eyes. None of this made any sense. Or maybe it did. If there really was a God, it all made perfect sense. The practicality of this entire series of events rested on the reality of God. Alex settled into the booth, turning so that he could rest his back against the wall.

"Alright. I'm ready to listen if you're willing to talk. Tell me about God and why on Earth you're forgiving me for something I can't forgive myself for."

38

Wynn pulled her hair back with a hair band and stared at the computer screen, willing her Literature paper to write itself. Her notes and in-depth outline were spread across the desk. Writing the paper was not really such a difficult task; the hard part was already done. She just had no motivation. Her ability to concentrate on anything had been stripped away by the events of the last two days.

"Alright. Snap out of it, Gwyneth Paige," she reprimanded herself. She positioned her hands on the wrist pad and tapped out the title she had settled on and her name. She smiled at the Times New Roman, 12-point font.

"There. That's a good start."

It took two hours to produce six pages of well-supported opinion. She was interrupted when someone knocked on her door. Ducky pushed it open and poked her head in.

"Not now," Wynn said, not bothering to look up. "I'm on a roll. Only two more pages to go. Come back sometime after dawn."

"Your brother's on the phone," Ducky announced, holding up the receiver, stretching the phone cord to its greatest length.

"Tell him I'm composing a great work of literary criticism and I haven't the time to conversate with him."

"Is conversate even a word?"

Wynn lowered her brows and thought for a moment. "I don't know, but if it isn't, it should be."

Ducky raised the receiver. "She's currently composing a, what was it again?"

"A great work of literary criticism," Wynn confirmed,

misspelling intelligence as she tried to talk and write at the same time.

"A great work of literary criticism and hasn't the time to conversate with you. Uh-huh. Alright. He says you can compose later. He needs to talk to you."

"Tell him my scholarly endeavors take precedence over trivial matters, so unless the matter of which he needs to speak is of an urgent nature, I must adamantly decline his request to converse with me. Converse! That's it; not conversate."

"Did you hear all of that?" Ducky asked. "Yeah, she's been reading Jane Austin. Well of course, she was an excellent author. She was British.

"He says it is of an urgent nature."

"Oh alright, alright." She finished typing a sentence and clicked save. The phone cord would not reach further than her doorway so she was forced to leave her computer. Ducky made a face at her as she relinquished the receiver.

"Hello, dearest, loveliest Gabriel," she cooed into the phone. Wynn walked into the kitchen and fetched a cup from the cabinet. Her brother snorted.

"For future reference never call a man lovely. It's disturbing," Gabe informed her. She nodded.

"Noted." She pulled the strawberry syrup and the gallon of skim milk from the refrigerator.

"You sound like you're in a good mood."

"I am. I got an A on my practicum test, my lit paper is nearly done, and I'm making strawberry milk." She squirted syrup into the glass until there was a thick, pink, puddle at the bottom. "So what is so very urgent that you would disturb me in the midst of my brilliant composition?"

"I'm taking Ducky to dinner on Friday."

Wynn frowned. "You interrupted me to tell me that?"

"No, but I just remembered it and wondered if you knew what her favorite flowers were."

"I don't know. Do you want me to ask her?" she offered, sloshing in the milk.

"No. I don't think roses for a first date, do you? I'll ask the florist."

"You're getting flowers from a florist? Wow."

"One of my residents is dating an interior design student whose sister owns a florist shop. She said she would get her sister to give me free flowers if I would tutor her boyfriend, my resident, in General Psych."

Wynn stirred her drink and then licked the syrup stuck to the spoon. "Sounds like a complicated arrangement. So cut to the chase, Boyo. What did you call me for?"

"Sit down first."

"I am," she lied, returning the milk to the fridge.

"No, you're not. Sit. I won't say anything until you do," Gabe threatened. She straddled the bar stool and sipped her milk.

"Alright. Spill it."

There was a pause.

"I went to the hospital today."

"Are you hurt? What happened? Why didn't you call me sooner?" she demanded. He chuckled.

"No. I went to Children's. To meet with Alex Chadwell."

She said nothing. She wasn't surprised. She had thought Gabriel might go through with it. He had such a compassionate heart. He was a much better Christian than she was. And that annoyed her.

"Wynn, ya there?"

"How did it go? Still think he's affected?" she wondered,

trying to sound as if she really didn't care one way or the other about Alex Chadwell.

"Yup. He was affected alright. He accepted Christ, Wynn."

Wynn was stunned by the news. Not in a million years had she expected it.

"Wynn?"

Well, if this didn't just top it all off. Anger squirmed within her. It would seem that Alex Chadwell's life was just perfect now. He was a doctor who came from money, probably had a mansion on a hilltop, and a model girlfriend. And now he had God's favor as well. She felt like a beaten prisoner who had just been given a last spiteful slap across the face.

"Wynn? Gwyneth Paige?"

"Yeah, Gabe."

"Are you alright? I thought the news would be exciting. See, good is coming from it all."

Wynn slumped on her stool. "Yeah, Gabe, it's just great. His wonderful life is now picture perfect."

"Wynn."

"He's got everything he needs now. He believes in God. He'll have no more worries."

"You believe in the same God, Wynn. And you know it's not that easy. You're not looking past your own hurt to see that he's been hurting, too. You should be ecstatic that he's accepted Christ," Gabriel rebuked. Wynn's fury boiled over.

"You can judge and condemn me all you want to, Gabriel. You hide behind that perfect, saintly image you've constructed, but this is me being real. This is me dealing with something that you can just shrug off. I've accepted what's happened. You're just trying to justify it all. You're trying to give what happened a purpose. I don't give a flying flip about what its purpose was. It happened. Now all I'm trying to do is get on with my life and this just keeps getting thrown back into my face."

"Why are you so angry? Why can't you and Dad learn that this wasn't an attack on you? God didn't set out to destroy you. What if this isn't even about you, Wynn?"

Wynn was crying now but she refused to let her brother hear her tears.

"God made it about me," she shot back. She took a shaky breath.

"I'm not angry because they're gone. I'm not even angry because Alex lived anymore. I'm angry and I'm hurt because every time things are beginning to go well, every time I'm trying my hardest to be a good person and move on I get slapped on the face again. Taking them away wasn't enough. God is using every chance He gets to hurt me. And then people like you and everyone else make me feel like I'm a horrible person because I can't get over it. I can't smile and lie like you have. I can't be a saint. I never have time to heal. Every time I get back up, I get knocked down again. And there you all stand, telling me how selfish and self-centered I am." She was shouting now, voicing the hurts and the truths she'd thought she had overcome. She was angry with God again. Would she never stop blaming Him?

Her brother remained silent as she struggled to stop her tears. Ducky had come into the room and stood by, her presence telling Wynn that she was there if she needed her.

"Wynn?"

"I don't want to talk about this anymore."

"Wynn, we have to talk about this. You're right. I have

no right to judge you and I never meant for it to seem that way."

Wynn sniffled and took the box of tissues that Ducky held out to her. She sighed.

"Gabe, I really don't want to talk about it anymore. I have to finish my paper and I have clinicals tomorrow. Please, let's drop it for now. I'll talk to you later. Here, here's Ducky." She shoved the phone into her friend's hands and left the kitchen. She didn't want to talk to Gabe or to Ducky or to anyone else. She stumbled down the hall, to her bedroom, and shut the door. She turned the lock.

The anger was already dissipating. She felt so selfish and petty. Depression and the self-loathing would come next. The cycle never ended, even when the longing for her family had. This is what God allowed. He let the hurt recycle itself. It didn't matter how many prayers she prayed, she couldn't overcome it. She sat down at her desk and let the tears fall.

39

"Steve, I need to talk to you," Alex told the man who had just opened the door. Steve looked surprised to see him and even more surprised at the greeting. He stepped back and opened the door wider. Alex crossed the threshold of the Perch's small but comfortable home. The tiny foyer was overflowing with cast off shoes and jackets hanging from hooks on the wall. Alex removed his black loafers, kicking them into the pile of footgear.

"We're having dinner. You're welcome to join us," Steve announced leading the way through the small living room toward the dining room.

"I didn't realize. I can wait in the car," Alex objected, already returning to fetch his shoes.

"Don't be stupid.

"Melissa, Abby we've got company," his host called. Chair legs scraped against the floor as the Perch women left the table to greet him. Steve's four-year-old daughter rounded the corner first. Her little face dimpled with a smile.

"Uncle Alex!" she squealed, flinging herself at his legs.

"Hello, Squirt."

Steve's petite wife followed her daughter, a hand on her round tummy. She waddled over. Melissa had always been a sweetheart. She smiled and reached to give Alex a hug.

"Hey there, Uncle Alex. How are you doing?" she wondered, her round face veiled with concern. It was obvious Steve had shared with her the conversation he had had with Alex. Alex didn't mind. These two had been the most faithful and genuinely caring friends he had ever had.

"I'm doing good. I didn't mean to interrupt—"

"Don't be silly. We're just having chicken casserole, but there's plenty. Come on and eat," Melissa commanded, wobbling back toward the kitchen. She smiled at her husband when he winked as she passed.

Steve lifted Abby onto his shoulders and followed his wife back to the table. A plate and cup was fetched from the oak cabinets before Alex could make another objection. Steve pushed him toward a padded chair.

"You can sit by me. I'm there." Abby pointed at a plastic Blue's Clues plate covered with casserole and green beans. Her father deposited her in her chair and she reached for her purple cup.

"I'm gonna have a bruver, Uncle Alex. Daddy says he's going to be littler than me. That's pretty little, huh? Mommy says he won't be able to talk to me for a little while. I don't know why. I'm awful nice to talk to."

The adults chuckled at this, but the mature little four-year-old did not see the humor.

"Daddy says Mommy will have to go to the hosbital. That's where the babies are d'livered. Do they come in white trucks like the mail?"

Alex had all he could do not to laugh at the serious question.

"Something like that," he confirmed. Abby scooped up a spoonful of green beans.

"I get to stay with Happy when my bruver's d'livered."

"An older couple from church offered to keep her. They have a cockatiel named Happy," Steve supplied, his eyes twinkling with amused pride over his daughter.

"He always rides on Abby's shoulder whenever we visit. She looks like a baby pirate."

"And he pooped on me," Abby inserted. Melissa was aghast as Alex sat choking on the casserole.

"Abigail, that was rude! We don't use that word in public, remember?" Melissa looked thoroughly embarrassed, but the two men were shaking with laughter.

"I'm sorry," Abby apologized, with a protruding bottom lip. "But he did. Right here," she felt compelled to add as she pointed out the location. Alex knew he would have to excuse himself if he didn't want to hurt Abby's feelings or encourage her with his laughter. Melissa came to the rescue.

"Abby, why don't you and I go watch VeggieTales while we finish our supper, so Uncle Alex can talk to Daddy?" she suggested, struggling to her feet. Alex felt guilty and tried to coerce Melissa to stay, but Abby had already been enticed.

"Yeah," Abby agreed, turning in the big chair and sliding off the edge. Steve stood and gathered the plates and cups and carried them to the living room. When he returned, he was grinning.

"I didn't mean to ruin your dinner. It never even occurred to me that it was suppertime," Alex apologized. Steve shrugged.

"You didn't ruin anything. I think Lissa really just wanted to get Abby away from the table before she continued discussing bird droppings.

"So, what's up?" he wondered, reclaiming his forsaken chair. As bad as Alex felt for arriving unannounced and unwelcome at dinnertime, he was excited about the news he had come to proclaim.

"Do you remember Wynn Redecke?"

"Yeah," Steve said slowly. Alex took a bite of his dinner

before continuing to speak.

"Well," he said around the mouthful, "her brother paid me a visit last night at the hospital."

Steve quirked his brow. "Her brother came to see you? Did he threaten you or something?"

Alex shook his head and shoveled in another forkful.

"You don't look at all upset. What happened?" Steve demanded.

"He came to tell me that he forgave me and to ask me to forgive him."

Steve looked shocked. Alex nodded.

"Yeah, that's about how I looked. I was blown away. I didn't get it. I thought he was out of his mind." Gabriel's words had amazed him. What all those Christians preached, Gabriel had put into practice.

"He helped me figure something out. He helped me see the evidence that there is a God. So much has been leading up to last night and it finally just all made sense."

Steve studied his friend's face. "Do you mean that you believe in God? That you believe in Christ's sacrifice and salvation?"

Alex had always been a skeptic. The more Steve had evangelized over the years, the more Alex had ignored him. But Steve had planted the seed. Some of what he had said had gotten through. Last night at the hospital, Gabriel had just reaffirmed all of Steve's stories and something had finally clicked. Through Gabriel's extension of forgiveness, Alex had finally understood God's capability to forgive.

He nodded. "Yeah. I still don't understand it all and I know almost nothing about the Bible or really about Christ, but I want to know. I'm willing to confess that He exists and is all He said He was. And if I'm confessing that I really have no choice but to accept His salvation."

Steve let out a whooping "Hallelujah!"

"Your salvation is a prayer come true, man. Lissa, Lissa, come in here!" Steve called, excitedly. Melissa entered the kitchen with a confused look on her face. Steve grabbed her around her extended waist and kissed her. She laughed at the sudden show of affection.

"What was that for?" she wanted to know. Steve grinned.

"Tell her, Alex."

"I accepted Christ last evening."

"That's wonderful! I'm happy for you, Alex," she told him sincerely.

"Like I told, Steve. I don't understand very much about it yet, only that God is real, Christ's sacrifice was real, and that He really does forgive."

Steve clapped him on the back. "Seems to me like a perfect place to start."

40

Neon lights flashing below her window colored the ceiling. City noises hummed from outside the glass. The sounds of passing cars, broken voices, and sirens had become her lullaby, but tonight the din only made Wynn feel hollow and cut off from the world. Her body felt tired and she didn't care if she fell asleep or woke up or made it to school or work on time. Tears gathered in her eyes. All she could think of was what a horrible person she was and how everyone must hate her. It was the beginnings of depression. She knew the feelings well. She wished she could stop them, make herself forget about meeting Alex Chadwell, forget the argument with Gabe—but she couldn't.

"Father," she whispered. "Please stop this. I don't want to go through this again."

Wynn turned again and sighed. She wouldn't be going to sleep this night. She stood up and started toward the kitchen. The apartment was dark. Wynn grabbed the phone and dragged it to the couch. Curling up on a cushion she dialed a number. Unwanted and unprovoked tears gathered in her eyes. She tried to wipe them away, but it was no use. The phone rang seven times.

"H'lo?" mumbled a sleepy voice from the other end.

"Miss Clara?" Wynn's voice sounded thin and teary.

"Gwyneth? Honey, it's one in the morning. What's happened? What's wrong?" Clara Beetle's voice was filled with concern. Wynn shook her head and the tears began to tumble down her cheeks.

"I'm sorry, Miss Clara. I just needed someone to talk to. It's happening again and I don't know how to stop it."

41

Wynn grimaced when a loud rumble echoed through the room.

"Hungry?" DeJanna asked, quirking a dark eyebrow.

"Starved." Wynn checked her watch, hoping her break would be coming up soon. Not that she was in any hurry to leave all the adorable newborns in the nursery. She just feared she would perish of starvation before too much longer.

"I think these past few days have been my favorite clinicals ever," DeJanna said as she paused in the paperwork she was filling out.

Wynn nodded and Helen, their charge nurse, smiled. "I hear that a lot from nursing students." She peered over the rim of her glasses at Wynn.

"Finish up that paperwork and take a lunch break."

"Thank you," Wynn said with exaggerated gratitude. Wynn set to work, completing the charting in a few minutes. She was closing the binder when someone walked by whistling the Andy Griffith Show theme song.

"Hello, Doc," Helen greeted with a friendly smile. Wynn looked up, expecting to be staring at a kindly obstetrician. Instead, Alex Chadwell had stopped mid-stride and mid-whistle just ahead of them. The puckered, whistle-smile melted from his face. Helen looked from the doctor to Wynn and back again.

Wynn was not sure how to react. It had been four days since they had met on the ball field and three days since her outburst at Gabe. In that time she had tried praying everything through, just as Clara Beetle had instructed her to do during their early morning phone conversation, but her prayers seemed to be bouncing off the ceiling and crashing back down on her head.

She narrowed her eyes. What was he even doing here at University Hospital, on the maternity ward? Was he stalking her or something?

Alex must have realized then that he was staring.

"Hi," he finally said. Helen and DeJanna were both looking at Wynn.

"See you in half an hour girls," Helen said, removing the large binder from Wynn's hands.

She busied herself with work and DeJanna took off while Wynn stuttered through an objection.

"Would you be willing to talk to me for a few minutes?" Alex asked, his eyes pleading. Wynn took a deep breath and tried to steady her topsy-turvy emotions. He took her silence as affirmation and he moved across the hall and stepped into an empty family lounge.

"God, what are You doing?" she demanded in a whisper, before following him. She stood rigidly with her hands buried in the deep pockets of her smock. Alex ran an agitated hand through his dark hair. He didn't meet her eyes. She spoke up before he could.

"What are you doing here?"

He gave a weak half smile. "Children's partners with University to give their residents time in a newborn nursery. I'm just starting this rotation."

Oh. Wynn cast a glance toward the ceiling, wondering how much pleasure God had taken in arranging this meeting.

"I wanted to apologize, Wynn, Gwyneth, uh, Miss Redecke. I—I, uh—" he looked up. "I really don't know what to say. I just know that we're not going to be able to avoid running into one another, especially when I start my rotation on the inpatient wards at Children's. It would be idiotic of me to ask if we could just forget or ignore what happened. Neither of us can do that. I need to know that it is not going to tear you up to see me walking down the hall."

Wynn stared at him, her mouth parted to reply. She felt confused. After four days of fighting off depression and anger and sadness, she now felt nothing. Where was the hatred that had burned her heart a few days earlier? Where was the resentment she had felt? Had Clara's prayers worked so quickly?

Facing him for the third time in seven years, she found she did not hate this man. She wanted to, but she didn't. Wynn continued to stare and he shifted uncomfortably under her gaze.

"Gabe told me about the other night and the decision you made," she finally said. A small, hesitant smile raised one side of Alex's mouth.

"I want so much to hate you," she told him, her voice raw. There was no surprise in his expression.

"You have every right to."

She looked away and turned to leave.

"Miss Redecke," he called out. She turned. He smiled at her, a sad smile that caused her heart to constrict.

"I'm sorry," he said simply. Wynn only looked at him. Then without a word, she sped from the room and down the hallway.

42

Alex watched the young woman retreat down the hall. It was very clear that she wanted to remain as far away from him as possible. He sighed. The meeting had been unexpected. This was his first day at this hospital on this ward. That she should be here completing clinicals at the very same time was more than coincidental

"God," he mumbled, "I'm still new at this. Am I supposed to thank you for that reunion? I guess things could have gone worse."

Praying still felt a lot like talking to himself. Steve and Melissa had given him a Bible and answered many of his questions. They had even prayed with him, but this belief thing was a lot harder than he had thought it would be. He was continually having doubts. What if God wasn't real? What if Jesus didn't die? But then assurance would rush through him and for a few moments he would be positive that there was a God. Right now was one of those assured moments.

He shook his head and sighed again. He had no idea how he was going to avoid Wynn for the rest of the afternoon. They were sure to pass one another in the halls several more time before the evening was ended. Perhaps he should—

Suddenly her words hit him. He looked back down the hall where she had disappeared. 'I want so much to hate you.' Alex felt emotion well in his throat. Gratitude radiated through him. God had worked another miracle. Despite her hurt, despite her anger, Wynn Redecke did not hate him.

43

Wynn opened the door to her brother on Friday night, but instead of letting him in the room, she stepped out into the hallway. She had just returned home from her clinicals two hours before and she had to report for work in two hours. Normally she would have spent her few hour break napping, but this evening she had something she needed to do.

"Ducky is still fixing her hair. I told her I would stall you," she told him with a hint of a smile. Gabe had been leaving her messages all week, but she had not returned his calls.

"I guess I've been acting like a selfish brat, huh?"

"Yes," Gabe agreed with the description. His curt confirmation surprised a laugh from her.

"But you were right. I have been judging you and telling you what you should be doing and feeling. I'm sorry, Wynn."

Wynn shrugged. The things he had said had been right. It had hurt to hear them from him, to have him constantly reprimand her.

"Maybe I've been using the accident as a crutch, an excuse for everything else that has gone wrong. It has been my justification for my selfishness and self-pity, the anger and the unforgiving." She sighed and stared at her bare feet. She glanced up at him.

"We studied the stages of grief in one of my Psych classes, but I keep circling through them all, over and over again. The depression is the worse. I can't control it. But now I'm being forced to confront it all—the accident, Alex, and myself. I know God is telling me I can't use grief as a crutch anymore."

Gabe reached to hug her, holding the tissue wrapped bouquet away so as not to crush it. Wynn squeezed her twin.

"Wynn, you know I love you, don't you? You know I'm praying for you?"

Wynn smiled. "Believe me. Your prayers are definitely getting through. And I love you, too."

"I'm glad you're talking to me again. I have to admit, I missed having my sis around annoying me," he teased after releasing her. Wynn chose not to reply to that jab.

"I'm sure Ducky's ready by now. The flowers are nice by the way. She'll love them," she assured him as she pushed open the door. Gabe followed her in. They could hear Ashleigh in the bedroom talking about styling spritz and hairspray. Ducky's reply was too quiet to hear.

"Sounds like I need to be stalled for a few more minutes," Gabe said. He looked awkward standing in the living room, dressed in dark jeans and a sweater, clutching the wildflower bouquet. He had never been uncomfortable in his sister's home before, but now it was his date's living room as well. Gabe had always been so confident and debonair. His ill-concealed anxiety made Wynn smile. He saw her face and returned the smile.

"You know I've got it bad when I'm nervous, yeah?" He sat down on the couch and laid the flowers on the purple chest. "Distract me. Tell me about clinicals or class or something."

Wynn sunk into the overstuffed chair that Ashleigh had recovered with grass green fabric. She tucked her legs under her and settled into the soft cushions.

"Well," she started slowly, "Professor Swackhammer was halfway through her lecture on Wednesday when a pair of pigeons landed on the windowsill. They cooed for the next half hour and she had to yell over them. She finally went to the window and pounded on the glass, trying to get them to fly away. They just sat there, very nonchalantly, and cooed louder. Nothing of interest happened in clinicals." She paused and played with the hem of her nursing smock. Gabriel didn't even notice she had stopped talking, so engrossed was he in his plans for the evening.

"I was at University doing clinicals yesterday. Al ... Dr. Chadwell was there beginning his rotation in Newborn Nursery."

He looked up then.

"He and I spoke for a few minutes alone. I told him I want to hate him."

Gabriel laughed.

"He's not what I expected. When I met him the other day, before I found out who he was, I thought he was a very likable guy," she confessed. Gabe nodded in agreement.

"If he hadn't been involved in the accident we could've been friends, I think," he said with a shrug. Wynn turned thoughtful.

"What ya thinking?" he pried.

"If he hadn't been involved in the accident, we probably would never have known him. You probably would not have led him to Christ," she commented. Gabe smiled.

"Now you're starting to think like Wynn again."

He glanced up and immediately rose to his feet. Wynn looked behind her, noting that Ducky had taken her fashion advice. She had borrowed a gauzy skirt from Wynn and wore a soft powder pink sweater with it. Ashleigh had pulled Ducky's dark hair back into a French braid.

"Hi," Gabe greeted her, remembering to snatch up the flowers and walk over to meet her.

"Hello," Ducky returned. Their shy awkwardness was comical and Wynn had all she could do not to giggle.

Gabe held out the bouquet. "These are for you."

Wynn clamped a hand over her mouth. She was sure Ducky's next line would be, 'Oh, they're beautiful.'

"They're lovely, Gabe. Thank you."

The giggle squeaked out. Then Gabe began to chuckle. Ducky laughed outright. Ashleigh looked confused.

"What's so funny?" Ashleigh demanded, fetching a vase from under the sink.

"We are," Ducky said, smiling in amusement. She handed over the flowers for Ashleigh to arrange in the vase.

"Are you ready to leave before my sister laughs at us some more?" Gabe wondered with a grin. He lifted Ducky's toffee-colored pea coat from the hook near the door, and held it for her to slip into.

"An excellent idea," she agreed, the unease gone. Gabriel, ever the charmer, offered his arm in Victorian fashion.

"Goodbye," he called to his lady's roommates. He held open the door for Ducky. After she slipped through, he winked at Wynn, before exiting and shutting the door behind him.

"They're so cute together," Ashleigh said as soon as the door was shut. Wynn nodded. They were.

"How're you doing, Wynn. You've been so busy for the past week, I haven't really spoken to you," the blonde asked settling onto the couch. Wynn considered the question.

"I'm doing fine, now. I've realized a lot of things in the past few weeks. Now if I can put it all together and finally allow God to fix things, I'll be doing great.

"Thanks, Ash, by the way."

Ashleigh blinked.

"For what?"

"For putting up with me. For being my friend through all of this."

Ashleigh smiled.

"Wynn, you have always amazed me. I can't even begin to imagine what I would have done in your situation. Even when you struggle with the depression, you always fight to come out of it." Ashleigh shifted in her seat and demonstrated her next words with her hands.

"I remember watching you when you were struggling the most. There was nothing I could do. It was like you were drowning and then all I could do was watch. But then you would latch onto something and hold on and fight 'til you overcame it. I've always admired you for that."

Wynn reached for a tissue as the seemingly endless flow of tears began again. Ashleigh's words revealed something that she had never realized.

"That's been my problem, I think. That's why it keeps happening over and over again. I would latch onto some*thing*. At first, it was my love for my dad and Gabe. Then my puppy love for Jeremy. It's been school and work and my future patients, even Miss Clara and church. I need to latch onto God and hold onto Him."

44

"Alex, I haven't stopped praising God since you called me Monday. I've been going around the house singing like a Pentecostal choir. Your father thinks I've finally lost my mind. It's just so wonderful!"

"It's wonderful that Dad thinks you've lost your mind?" Alex quipped.

"No. That you've become a Christian. Are you going back to Living Branch? It was a good place to grow, Alex, I think. And there were several people about your age," his mother reminded.

"Steve invited me to go to his church, but I'm still considering Living Branch. I may try them both for a little while," Alex said into the phone, shrugging as if his mother could see him. When he had called her Monday night, she had been crying so hard he could barely understand her. Now she sounded elated.

"I was so surprised, Alex. I mean I always believed you would find God, but for Him to use the Redeckes—it's a miracle, you know. I just never would have guessed.

"You said that Gabriel Redecke is doing well. How is Gwyneth taking it all, do you think?" Joan wanted to know. Alex, who had been copying Scripture onto note cards when his mother called, tapped his pencil eraser on the pine tabletop.

"I'm not sure, Mom. I can't figure her out. Wynn was, I don't know. She seemed confused and surprised."

"She's been through a lot, so try to be understanding. She lost four people," She reminded softly. Alex felt the strong twinge of guilt, but it was replaced with compassion.

"I wish I could help her, Mom, but because of the role I played in all this, there's really nothing I can do."

"You can pray for her," his mother suggested. Alex nodded again.

"I'm still learning how to pray. Sometimes I feel like I'm talking to myself and sometimes I feel like I'm too lowly for God to listen to me."

"He always listens, Alex, even when you doubt He's there. And you're not too lowly for God to listen. He loves you and has accepted you as His son.

"Alex, Hon, I hate to end this but I am meeting your father for lunch, and you know how he hates to be kept waiting."

Alex knew very well. Punctuality was one of his father's many obsessions.

"Tell Dad I said hello. Tell him to give me a call. I haven't talked to him in a month and a half," Alex said, knowing full well he would have to be the one to do the calling.

"I will. You're coming home for Thanksgiving still, aren't you?"

"Are Mamaw and Aunt Julie cooking?"

"Yes. You know I don't cook Thanksgiving dinner since I tried to cook the turkey in the microwave and the thing blew up," his mother answered. Alex grinned.

"I'll be there, then."

"Good. I love you, Hon."

"Love you, too, Mom. Bye."

Alex hung up the phone and set it to the side. Busby was chasing his tail in the living room. The tail was winning—he hadn't caught it yet. Alex suddenly had the urge to take a walk. He had to be at the hospital that evening, but he had nothing to do until then. He snatched the leash from beside the back door.

"Come on, Boy. You and I are going to take a walk. Maybe we'll meet up with a pretty girl with a lady Poodle."

Busby was ecstatic at the prospect or maybe it was just the promise of a walk that had him wiggling with joy. Alex leashed him and grabbed a light jacket from his messy coat closet. He locked the front door and started down the sidewalk. The sky was free of clouds and the sunshine warmed the early November air. The maintenance crew was gathering the withered leaves from the manicured lawns of Maple Grove's congruent condominiums. Every yard displayed a young Maple growing on the right side and box bushes and mums crowding the paved stoop. Busby's nose was to the ground, his tail swishing back and forth in delight.

"God, thanks for this gorgeous day," Alex whispered. The thanksgiving rolled off his tongue without conscious thought. He smiled when Busby's ears perked up.

"No, I wasn't talking to you," he informed the pup. Busby barked and jerked the leash so suddenly that Alex did not have time to tighten his grip. The dog darted across the street, the leather leash trailing behind him. Alex watched him run for a second before realizing that he had to go after him. Busby disappeared around a corner as Alex sprinted after him. He rounded the corner, searching the streets for his dog. He saw the half-grown pup dashing across clipped lawns, chasing a black and white cat. Following the dog at high speed, was a woman. Many paces behind hobbled a stooped figure in a bright purple dress and navy overcoat.

"Stop, stop, stop!" she yelled out, exasperated that no one, cat, dog, or woman, was listening to her. Alex began whistling for his pet, running after the assorted sprinters.

The cat finally stopped, raising its striped tail. Busby halted a few feet away, barking viciously.

"Oh, no," Alex groaned. *That* wasn't a cat.

"Busby," he shouted. The younger woman caught the dog around the neck, dragging him back. She and the dog toppled over, Busby landing on top. Enchanted with his human rug, he began covering the woman's face with slobbery kisses. The elder woman scooped up the skunk just as Alex arrived on the scene.

"Dr. Chadwell!"

"Alex Chadwell?"

"Wynn? Clara?"

These exclamations were shouted at practically the same time as all three humans froze. Alex was the first to recover. With a hand on the scruff of the dog's neck and an arm around his back end, Alex lifted Busby off the stunned Wynn Redecke. She just stared at him for a good long moment. Finally, she burst into laughter. Clara followed suit, her shrill cackling mingling with the younger woman's breathless chortle. Finally, Alex saw the humor in the whole situation and joined them.

"Oh, good heavens!" Clara wheezed. She put a hand to her head and squinted. "I laughed so hard my head hurts. Whew!

"Well Alexander Chadwell, what're you doing here?" she demanded, stroking the hair of her startled skunk.

"I live here. What are you doing with a skunk?"

Clara Beetle looked down at her malodorous pet as if the better question would be: why doesn't everyone own a skunk?

"Oscar? Oh, he's been my friend for years. Skunks make wonderful pets, much better than cats. I detest cats. He couldn't have sprayed your dog. I had his stink removed.

"You live here, huh? I live three streets over," she informed him. "And how do you know Gwyneth?"

Alex realized then that Wynn was still on the leaf-covered ground witnessing the conversation. He took Busby's leash and dropped him to his paws. He reached a hand out to her. She took it and allowed him to pull her to her feet.

"Thank you," she said, jerking her hand away. Busby immediately jumped on her, begging for a pat.

"Busby, off," Alex commanded, but it did no good. The pup was enamored.

"You want me to pet you after you tackled me and covered me with drool?" Wynn demanded playfully. She scratched the dog behind the ears and on his neck still thick with puppy fat.

"I'm sorry. He's never run off before or chased a ca—I mean, a skunk. He's never even barked before today. Busby, off. Leave the lady alone." Alex pulled the capricious canine back.

"He's alright. I like dogs. This is the puppy that Anna named hers after?" she questioned, her eyes bright with a smile. He nodded surprised that she knew about Anna's christening her stuffed animal after his dog. Clara cleared her throat.

"You didn't answer my question. I wanted to introduce the two of you and you're already introduced. It just puts a damper on all my plans."

"Al—, um, Dr. Chadwell is the man you wanted me to meet?" Wynn wanted to know. Clara nodded, patting Oscar's head so hard that he nodded, too.

"But he's, he's—" she stopped and clamped her mouth shut.

"He's what?" Clara pressed. Alex steeled himself for the accusation.

"The man I was telling you about earlier this week, Miss Clara," Wynn finally said, her eyes conveying a meaningful look. Clara Beetle's eyes and mouth formed three similar circles.

"You mean he—you were and now you've—and well, good gracious, the good Lord works in mysterious ways." She turned her faded, gray eyes heavenward. Her whole face wrinkled and seemed to fold in on itself when she squinted.

"I just don't understand you, Lord, but I don't reckon I need to. You just never know what He's going to do next." She gave the two younger people a pointed look. Neither one spoke.

Alex noticed that Wynn would not look at him. Her cheeks were pink making the splattering of freckles on her nose stand out. She was really a very attractive woman he decided. Her hair was dark brown seasoned with strands of red. The sunlight caught on the threads of copper giving her tresses a fiery affect. Her long lashed, green eyes competed with her hair as her best feature. She was taller than average—the top of her head reached his nose. And Busby liked her.

"This is all a bit awkward, isn't it?" Clara said. She glanced at Alex, her look kind but firm. She was hinting that he should disappear.

"I'm sorry that Busby chased after your—Oscar. I'll let you finish your walk now. Bye."

He whistled to his dog. Busby whined and looked to Wynn. She smiled and patted him on the head.

"Bye, Busby," she said, shooing him away. The lovesick pup finally relented to his master's tugs on the leash. Alex offered the women a half smile before turning and dragging his dog across the street. Busby had to stop and bark at a Lincoln Towncar before he would allow himself to be relocated. Alex rolled his eyes. Now that the dog knew he could bark he would be yapping at everything in sight. Alex tugged the leash.

"Hush up, Pup. You can't scare it away. That car doesn't care that you can bark." Busby looked up at him, then woofed once more for good measure.

The two were rounding the corner when Alex heard someone call his name.

"Dr. Chadwell."

He turned.

"Alex," he corrected automatically. Wynn had crossed the street and stood near a slender tree, a safe fifteen paces away. A glance told him that Clara and Oscar were slowly recovering the road to their home.

"I wanted to tell you—actually I feel as if I *need* to tell you—that I don't blame you anymore for what happened," she said quickly, as if she had to get it out before she changed her mind.

He had not expected this. Alex felt something stir inside him.

"Thank you," he simply said. She nodded and blinked hard. She looked as if she were going to cry. "Wynn, I am sorry. I wish I could do more than offer apologies."

She sniffled and forced a smile. "You have." She took a step backwards.

"I have to go."

He nodded, not bothering to say goodbye. He watched her jog away to meet up with her elderly friend. Taking a deep breath, he looked up at the sky.

"God, I don't know why you're being so good to me after all I've done. Thank you for Wynn's forgiveness. And, God, help her through this. Don't let me cause her to lose her faith in you."

45

"You look like you could use a cup of tea. You have too much going on right now, Gwyneth," Clara said in a displeased tone as she washed her hands at the kitchen sink. Wynn snorted. That was the understatement of the century.

"Have you had any sleep?"

"I fell asleep when I got home at seven-thirty and slept until two. After I leave, I'll go home, finish some homework, and sleep until ten. Then I'll get ready for work."

Clara shook her head. Wynn smiled her reassurance.

"I'm fine, Miss Clara, really. This was my last week at the nursing home and I only have two months left of this quarter. The next two quarters will be much lighter. I'll have only nursing classes and work."

"And church and clinicals and graduation preparations and finding a new place to live and then you're so worried about your father and this Alex Chadwell thing has you upset. I'm worried about ya, honey," Clara said as she filled the copper teakettle with water and slid it over the glass top stove. She took the seat across from her guest.

"When you told me earlier that you had met the boy that was in the accident with your mother and that he was a doctor at Children's I should have put two and two together. But of all the people in this world, it had to be him. After all the plans I had for the two of you."

"Miss Clara!"

"Well. He's such a nice boy. Imagine, him living just a few streets away from me."

"It seems the more I try to avoid him, the more places

he shows up," Wynn said with a wry smile. Clara quirked a penciled eyebrow.

"Maybe God's trying to tell you something."

Wynn nodded. "I think He was and I think I finally listened. When I ran across the street to speak with Alex, I told him that I didn't blame him anymore. Now maybe he'll leave me alone," she joked. She had meant what she said. She did not blame him. She could even praise God for his salvation.

"Well, I'm proud of ya, honey. After all that you told me this morning, I can see that you're moving on, you're growing and that's a prayer answered." Clara rose to fetch the whistling kettle. Wynn stood and pulled two coffee mugs from the corner cabinet. She brought out the honey and milk while Clara filled the cups with hot water and dropped the tea bags in to steep.

"He's just so dadburned handsome," Clara suddenly burst. Wynn laughed.

"And he's good. I can tell. You can't be a children's doctor and not be a good person," Clara continued, carrying the mugs to the table. "Well, I suppose the Lord knows what He's doing." She sighed. Wynn couldn't help but smile. Poor Clara. She was an avid matchmaker and this new development would hamper her plans considerably. She would have to find a new prospect for Wynn and would probably start looking for a sweetheart for Alex, as well.

"Miss Clara, you'll just have to set your sights on another handsome man."

Clara Beetle threw her hands in the air. "No, I quit. This has just broken my heart. The good Lord knows how I am. He should have never let me lay eyes on Alex Chadwell. He knew I'd pick him out for you and He let me meet him anyway."

Wynn laughed again. "So this is all God's fault?"

Clara took the plastic honey bear and gave him a hard squeeze.

"Fault is much too strong a word. It's all God's doing, and I suppose that should be comforting, since He does everything for our good. But I just don't think I can ever do any heart matching again. I'll mourn this match until the end of my days.

"By the way how are Octavia and Gabriel doing? I have been trying to get those two to notice one another for a year now."

46

Alex smiled at the young woman with whom he was engaged in conversation. He guessed her to be in her late twenties. She had accidentally bumped into him when he was leaving the church pew. When he had apologized and introduced himself she had politely returned the introduction and asked him what he had thought of the sermon. He had found it interesting and said as much.

"Reverend Kline is an excellent minister. His studies have been extensive. He can read Greek, Hebrew, Aramaic, and Latin.

"So what do you do, Mr. Chadwell?" she asked with a friendly smile.

"I'm a doctor in residency at Children's Hospital. And you?"

"Oh, I'm an English professor."

Alex inwardly groaned. English.

"I write in my spare time. Nothing terribly exciting, just children's stories and a few essays. I dabble in poetry," she went on. Alex nodded more for the sake of politeness than true interest. Just then, Abby ran up and pounced on him.

"I made a macaroni necklace in Sunday School and I gave it to Mommy and she liked it. Daddy said to come get you 'cuz you needed to be rescued," she chattered as he lifted her into his arms. His face heated in embarrassment for the young woman. Her lips thinned and color burned beneath her makeup. Her look was apologetic.

"It was nice to have met you, Dr. Chadwell," she managed and turned on her heel.

"You too," Alex called after her retreating figure.

He groaned. Abby was smiling broadly, happy to have completed her mission.

"You just got me into trouble, Squirt."

"I'm sorry," she said with a pout. He tickled her side and made her smile again. He found Steve waiting for him at the back of the Sanctuary.

"I sent Abby to chase away Miss Toliver. Once she starts talking she never stops," he said with a grin. Alex gave him a sarcastic look.

"Yeah, thanks." He related Abby's little speech and Ginny Toliver's reaction. Steve groaned and reached for his daughter.

"I forget that she'll repeat everything you say. Come here, kiddo. Next time I'll send Melissa. I bet Ginny is mortified. She really wasn't flirting—she just talks a lot," Steve explained, seriously.

"I don't know whether I should apologize or let it go," Alex said, searching the crowd of parishioner's for Ginny's honey blonde hair. She must have made a run for it because she was nowhere to be seen.

"You didn't do anything wrong. I'll take care of it. I'm the one who sent Abby to rescue you."

"I'm getting off to a great start here," Alex mumbled. He had found the sermon very interesting and the people were all very friendly, but he had found himself wishing he were attending Living Branch. He had liked Pastor Polk's intimate form of preaching. He had preached like one who knew God well. He had not used a lot of impressive sounding, theological terms or tried to delve too deeply into the intellectuality of the Bible. And the music! Living Branch had had a very good band, led by a pretty soprano, but the praise had been genuine. There had been nothing ostentatious about their worship. Here there was an orchestra and a choir, a praise band, a youth band, a dance team, and a worship team. It seemed a bit much in Alex's opinion.

"You look disappointed," Steve commented. Alex shrugged.

"This wasn't what I was expecting. I don't mean to judge or insult, but I felt like I was watching a show today instead of attending a worship service."

A thoughtful look covered Steve's face. "Melissa has said that before. I suppose the lights and the screens and the music can be either a tool or a distraction. When they distract you away from God, they lose their purpose."

"I think at this point I need as little distraction as possible. I think I'll look around for a while. Maybe this is where I'm supposed to be, but right now it just doesn't feel right."

Steve nodded in understanding. He took no offence at his friend's words. He was actually glad to see that Alex was searching for a place where he could grow and focus his attention on God.

"Go get your wife. I'm taking you out to dinner," Alex commanded his friend.

"You need a girlfriend. Even things up," was Steve's random comment as he scanned the dwindling crowd for Melissa. She was weaving her way toward them so he stood still. Alex chuckled. He often felt like the odd man out when he spent time with his married friends. He had had girlfriends aplenty over the years, some he still spoke to. It had been more than a month, however, since he had been on a date.

"I was trying to get me one and you sent Abby to

rescue me," he joked, loosening his tie. Melissa joined the threesome just then.

"Nope. I know you much better than that. She isn't your type. You always liked the girls that played hard to get. The sweet, little, shy ones. Me," he put an arm around his wife's waist and pulled her close, "I like the gorgeous, brilliant, pregnant ones."

"Sounds like I missed out on an interesting conversation," Melissa said, pecking her husband on the cheek.

"Daddy said Uncle Alex needs a girlfriend," Abby filled her in. Melissa smiled. It was obvious she agreed, but she did not voice the opinion.

"I keep forgetting that little ears hear everything," Steve said, swinging his daughter onto his shoulders.

"Yes, they do. So what are the plans for the afternoon? There's not another softball game that you forgot to tell me about is there?"

"Not unless Porter forgot to tell me," Steve replied with a shrug. Abby giggled as her father's shrugging shoulders bounced her into the air.

"I'm taking the Perch family to dinner," Alex informed her. "So get in your car and follow me. I'm starving."

47

Wynn's cell phone was buried in her book bag. Digging through the crumpled papers, heavy books, and writing utensils was proving a fruitless venture.

"Keep ringing," she instructed the phone. "Oh, there's my calculator. Ah-ha!"

She pulled out the ringing piece of equipment and flipped it open.

"Hello?"

"Howdy!"

A smile spread across Wynn's face. She lugged her bag to a bench and sat down.

"Jeremy! Hi! How are you?"

The deep voice on the other end of the line chuckled. "I'm good. You sound happy today."

"I am happy today," she confirmed.

"Things are going good then?" Jeremy asked and this time Wynn chuckled.

"God is going good." She leaned back against the seat. "You would not believe what has happened in the past few weeks."

"Try me," he challenged.

Wynn glanced at her watch. She had only thirty minutes before her next class and needed to stop by the library, but it wasn't often that Jeremy called.

"Well, where do I start? I met the guy who was in the car accident with my family."

Jeremy was silent.

"Jeremy, are you there?"

"Yeah. Are you serious? How are you, really?"

Wynn smiled. Jeremy knew her well. He had always been a good friend. He had helped her through the hardest years. He had always encouraged her, pushed her, and offered a shoulder to cry on. He had lost his father to cancer in junior high—he had been able to understand her hurt when her other high school friends could not.

"I'm really well. At first, it was the same old cycle starting all over again, but this time, I don't know, God took over. I have so many people praying for me."

"So what happened? How did you meet him again?" Jeremy wanted to know.

"At a softball scrimmage. He figured it out first and told me who he was." She quickly related a brief version of their meetings.

"Wynn, I wish I could be there for you. Did you tell Gabe?"

"I did and that's the most amazing part. You know my brother. He went to the hospital and met with him. He told him he forgave him. Gabe ended up leading Alex, I mean, Dr. Chadwell, to Christ."

Jeremy's laugh was laced with surprise and his voice filled with admiration. "Good ol' Gabriel. Wow. That is awesome!"

"Yup," Wynn agreed. Her smile was full of pride for her brother.

"What about your dad? How did he take the news?"

The smile melted. She felt suddenly cold, despite her thick jacket and the warmth of the late October sun.

"I haven't told him yet. I hadn't even thought about telling him," she answered. She had not thought of what her father's reaction would be. "Do you think I should?"

Her friend did not answer for a long moment. "How

would he respond? Would the news bring him toward the Cross or push him further away?"

Wynn thought about the question for a long moment. "I don't know. After the accident, it was like Daddy was replaced by a stranger. He holds Gabe and me at a distance. We've never been able to get close to him again. It's like we really don't even know him."

"I don't know, Wynn. Everybody handles loss so differently. When we lost Dad, Mom clung to us, almost suffocated us. I got angry. Jen got depressed. We all responded to things in different ways.

"I don't know what I would do if I were you, Wynnie."

Wynn sighed, the happy feeling from moments ago replaced with an empty one.

"Wynn?"

Wynn shook her head and forced the feeling away. She had given this situation up to God. Was she going to trust Him with it or not?

"God will take care of it. I won't worry about it.

"So what's up with you? How's life in California?" she demanded of her friend.

"Great. I actually have news. Do you remember Maygen?"

Wynn nodded as if he could see. "Of course I do. She's the incredibly sweet, breathtakingly beautiful girlfriend you're always talking about."

"Well, now she's my incredibly sweet, breathtakingly beautiful fiancée," Jeremy announced, pride and happiness evident in his tone. Wynn's smile returned.

"Congratulations! That's wonderful! Does this mean I finally get to meet her?"

"The wedding's in July, here in California. You're at the

top of the guest list. Maygen's looking forward to meeting you, too. You're going to get along great."

"I'm so excited for you, Jeremy! I want an engagement picture as soon as you have them made."

Jeremy groaned and followed up with a chuckle. "Dude! You're worse than my mother."

"Dude?"

"A bit of California vernacular for you.

"Well, Wynn, I'll let you go. I'm sure you have some class to run off to."

"Quite right, you are," Wynn said with an oft-practiced British accent. She glanced at her watch as she stood and slung her bag over her shoulder. "I have fourteen minutes to get across campus. It was so wonderful to hear from you, though. Give my best wishes to Maygen."

"Will do. Have fun in class. And Wynn? You'll be in my prayers. God'll let you know what to do about your dad."

Wynn nodded. A thought surfaced in her mind, prompting her to make a request of her friend. "Thanks. Jeremy?" she hesitated. "Could you maybe—this may sound strange—but could you pray for Dr. Chadwell, too? He's a new believer and his life is being turned upside-down all over again, as well."

She could hear the smile in Jeremy's voice. "Yeah. Yeah, I'll definitely pray for him. You amaze me, Wynn. Keep it up."

48

Wynn lounged on the couch, flipping through the channels. Her turkey TV dinner sat on the coffee table. The gravy was starting to congeal. She yawned and stretched her legs out.

The Macy's Thanksgiving Day Parade was over. She had no interest in football. She had watched *It's a Wonderful Life* so many times she could quote it word-for-word.

"What a wonderful way to spend Thanksgiving," she mumbled, reaching for her mug of apple cider. Ducky and Ashleigh had both traveled home for Thanksgiving break. Even Gabe had gone home to spend the holiday with their family. But Wynn had to work. Gabe had promised to bring back leftovers and to try to convince their father to travel north for a visit. Ron Redecke had not visited Cincinnati since he had deposited his children off at their respective universities.

Wynn checked her watch. Her family would have just finished dinner and would be heading to the livingroom and den and spare bedrooms to sleep it off. She reached for the phone, punched the speed dial and counted the rings. *One, two, three-*

"Hello?"

"Chelsea?" she asked the young voice that answered.

"Nope."

Wynn waited a moment for the undisclosed relative to reveal her identity, but she didn't.

"Um, who is it then?"

"It's Brittany. Is this Wynn?"

"Yes. How are you, Britt?" she demanded of her cousin.

"Good. What're you doing?"

Wynn glanced around her messy apartment. "I'm eating some kind of processed turkey product, drinking instant apple cider, and staring mindlessly at the television screen."

"Sounds like fun," Brittany said with a laugh.

"Yeah. Loads. So what am I missing?"

"Do you really want to know?"

"No. It'll only make me feel even sorrier for myself.

"Is my dad around?"

"Yeah, hold on. Uncle Ron!" she screamed. Wynn cringed and pulled the receiver away from her ear.

"Hello?"

"Daddy?"

"Hello, Sweetheart. How're you doing?"

Wynn considered the question. Other than her current minor bout of self-pity, all was well. She was happier than she had been in a very long time. Her grades were holding steady, she had only two weeks left before the quarter ended, and, despite her hectic schedule, she enjoyed her job.

"I'm doing great, Daddy. How are you?"

"I'm fine, Wynn. I wish you could have come down. We all miss you."

"I wish I could have made it, too. Sitting here is about to drive me batty. I don't even have any homework to keep me occupied. I'll probably end up cleaning this place up and taking a nap before work.

"How's Podie?"

Her father chuckled. "She's a brat. She bawls every morning around seven, then at noon, and at five for her bottle. She's spoiled."

Ron finished speaking and fell silent. The quiet had a strange feel—a hesitant feel.

"Daddy?" Wynn prompted.

"I've been thinking a lot lately, Wynnie. I know you've been worried. I've made it harder on you, and I'm sorry for that. Gabe and I talked last night. He told me about Alex Chadwell."

Wynn sucked in a breath and waited. It had been weeks since she had run into him. What would her father think of the encounter?

"I'm real proud of you and Gabe for what you did. You're both stronger than I am." They were good words but his voice was strained. He paused. Wynn was surprised when he chuckled.

"Gabe would make a good preacher. He sure knows how to annoy the tar out of a person. He made me furious. If he was younger I would have taken a belt to him," he said. Wynn could just see him shaking his head, a small, proud smile on his face.

"Yeah, he's good at that. But you were a great preacher once. He learned it all from you," she dared to say. Her father made no reply.

"Do you remember the time Gabe and Caleb played preacher. Chassity and I were the choir. We tried to baptize Hope. She was just a baby and—"

"Wynn. Not yet. Maybe sometime soon, but not yet.

"I think your Aunt Layla wants to talk to you. I love you, Wynn."

"Love you, too, Daddy."

49

"Go, go, go, go, go!"

"Aww! Come on!"

"What was that?"

"He could do better than that!"

Alex slapped his hand to his forehead as the replay showed the painful tackle in slow motion. The camera had zoomed in so close the audience could see the spit flying from the running back's mouth. All the men in the room groaned in unison. He sat on the edge of the couch cushion, his forearms resting on his thighs. His two uncles sat beside him, both with beer bottles in their hands. The proximity of the alcohol made the temptation nearly unbearable. Last year Alex had given in and had a drink. This year he had more than his own willpower to rely on. His prayers were something like, "God, don't let me want it. Don't let me give in. Nope, I don't want it. Don't let me do it."

He focused his attention on the screen. He missed football. His muscles were taut with the desire to be playing the game again.

"You wish it was you playing, don't ya, Al?" his father demanded from his place in the armchair.

Alex's eyes left the widescreen TV. He had turned down the chance to play college ball. He had been better at baseball, but with enough determination, he could have made it in football. Football had always been the one thing he and his father could agree on.

"Yeah," he confessed. "I do."

"You could have been famous, Alex," his cousin, Lance,

threw out. "If I were you, I would have kept playing. I'm goin' to."

Alex nodded. Yes, Lance would keep playing. What sane teenager would give up the chance to go pro? His entire family knew the answer to that one. A teenager who had held the hand of a dying five-year-old. Hope was the reason he was a doctor. Even when he had tried to forget her, she was the motivation that drove him.

"Yup, could have made the hall of fame," he said with good-humored sarcasm. He didn't regret being a doctor. He liked the work he did. God had had other plans even before Alex had believed there was a God.

"Being a doctor wasn't such a bad choice, though," his grandfather piped up as a commercial for margarine came on. He was dozing in the oversized leather chair in the corner. When his eyes would close, his white mustache would start twitching. When Alex and his cousins were younger, they used to be amazed by their grandpa's dancing facial hair.

"Yeah, doctors are much better than lawyers," his uncle Gene said. Darren Chadwell's eyes narrowed.

"Which are both better than real estate agents," he replied.

"Hey now, I was just kidding," Gene objected, pointing the neck of his bottle in his older brother's direction. Darren had always been quick to remind his younger brothers how successful a lawyer he was and how inferior their professions were to his. Greg, the youngest of the competitive Chadwell brothers, owned a photography studio with his wife.

"So how's it going up there in the big city," Greg asked his nephew, diverting the attention from his older brothers' sparring match.

"Good. I like what I'm doing. I have a lot of good friends there," he replied, stretching his legs forward and leaning back against the seat.

"How did you manage to get off for Thanksgiving?" Brad, his aunt's boyfriend, wanted to know.

"Shut up. The game's back on," his father suddenly commanded. All the men's attention returned to the television. Alex smiled grimly. His father was always obeyed.

When the opposing team scored another touchdown, Alex could stand no more.

"I can't take this," he exclaimed, grimacing at the sportscaster's recap. "This is too painful."

He climbed around his cousins sprawled out on the floor and headed toward the spacious kitchen. The women had vacated the room some time before. He could hear the mixture of feminine voices coming from the living room. He knew his cousins, Gina and Lora, would be in his old room watching the game. They were football fanatics, but disliked the masculine company gathered in the great room.

Alex unwrapped a corner of the plastic wrap that covered the carved turkey. He pulled out a hunk of meat and bit into it. The pies were sitting on the counter waiting to be eaten. He was tempted to slice a sliver of his grandmother's chess pie. His mother would kill him if he stole a piece before the appointed time. Desert was always promptly served after three, allowing everyone plenty of time to digest Thanksgiving dinner.

He grabbed a can of soda from the fridge, pulled his tennis shoes on, and went outside. The air was frosty and wet with unfallen rain. The awning had been stretched over the patio. The slate had been swept clean of dead leaves.

He crossed the patio and stepped out onto the spongy ground. The lawn was flawless. His mother's English garden still held a few of its late fall blooms. The dead foliage had been cleaned away, the leaves had been taken away as soon as they fell from the tree. Gardening had always been his mother's favorite past time. She managed her flower garden and the landscaping around the house while his father hired a company to mind the lawn. Not once had Alex had to cut the grass at his house. Some day, after his residency and after he found someone, he would buy some land, build a house, and buy a lawnmower.

He squinted up at the overcast sky. He was amazed at how life went on as usual. He had assumed when he put his faith in God that his life would be torn apart and rearranged, but most things were still the same. He still felt the same longings, had the same goals and dreams, was tempted to commit the same sins. His salvation had not miraculously settled his differences with his father or perfected the bad things in his life. He still found himself allowing his eyes to wander, craving alcohol, and letting a few choice words slip out when Busby made a mess all over the house or a driver cut him off in rush hour traffic. Through all of this, he felt a peace he had never before experienced. He recognized his shortcomings as sins and felt repentance. He felt assured of God's forgiveness and love, but he still felt as though he were missing something. God did not expect perfection, but Alex did feel that God was expecting more of him.

He glanced back toward the house when a boisterous shout sounded from the great room. He realized that since the accident he had withdrawn himself from people. He had always handled life on his own, by his own terms. He had never relied on others. And even since accepting Christ he had been trying to continue in his old routine alone, without the support and encouragement of Christian friends. Steve and Melissa were his only friends who shared his faith. He had visited several churches over the last weeks, but had not settled into a church family yet. Not only had he not sought the advice and support of other believers, but he had really not even searched the Scriptures or prayed over the decisions he had made concerning his life. He had invited Christ into his heart, but not into his life.

Alex was beginning to understand that faith required humility and dependence on God. He remembered Pastor Polk's sermon on Joseph. This was why God had allowed Joseph to be brought so low. He had to learn that he wasn't strong enough to make it on his own. He had to be willing to rely on God completely.

A lone leaf, one of the last survivors still clinging to the dried tree branches, fluttered toward the ground. He bent to pick it up, turning it over in his hand. The skin was leathery, tough. It had held out, but in the end it had died like the rest. He sighed.

"Alright, God. I get it. You want every part of my life. My plans, my dreams. You want me to place control in your hands. I'll try, God. This isn't going to be easy for me, but I'll try."

50

Wynn had decided to splurge a little and treat herself to some ice cream. Finals week had just ended and her stress level was still elevated. She would not breathe easy until she received her grade report in the mail.

She accepted the giant waffle cone and thanked the young man behind the counter. She took a seat in one of the wrought iron chairs at a table in the middle of the crowded food court. She dropped her numerous bags on the floor at her feet. She was finding that shopping alone was a bit boring. She had invited Ducky to join her, but her friend had plans for the evening. She and Gabe were having dinner at her parent's small mansion in Indian Hills. Ashleigh had also received the invitation but had had to work. Neither had any of Wynn's other friends been available to frivolously spend the evening. Even Clara Beetle had had plans. Wynn had not let the lack of company deter her.

She glanced again at the overflow of bags pooled in the floor and wondered how on earth she would get it all home on the bus. She had let Ashleigh borrow her car since Ashleigh's vehicle had refused to start when she hopped in to head to work. Wynn looked at her watch. If she could wander around the mall for another three hours, Ashleigh would be off work and could pick her up. She could see a movie. She twisted in her seat so that she could see the theatre marquee.

Wynn was deliberating over the listings when she had the skin-crawling sensation that someone was staring at her. She looked up. A group of middle school students had commandeered several nearby tables, an elderly couple sat in a corner, a family with a screaming infant and a battling brother and sister filled a booth table. It was a tall man standing at the Subway counter who was staring at her. He was with a pretty, young woman who had also turned to look at Wynn. Wynn felt her face warming as she recognized him. She had not seen him in a month and a half, since Busby had chased poor Oscar.

Alex Chadwell looked as surprised to see her as she was to see him. For a moment, neither made any move. She finally offered a small smile before looking away. She inwardly groaned when Alex approached the table, leaving his date at the counter.

"Hello," he said softly. She looked up and forced a smile.

"Hello."

"How are you?" he asked.

"I'm very well, thank you."

Alex nodded and ran a hand through his hair. It was a nervous gesture, Wynn noted.

"May I speak to you or is it better that I didn't?"

Wynn thought about the request. She felt no anger or pain at the sight of him. In fact, she was flustered. She glanced at the brunette at the counter. She could not imagine what Alex would have to discuss with her while he was supposed to be on a date.

Alex must have followed her gaze because he glanced toward the lovely lady.

"She and I attend a Bible study together. The group decided to come to the mall after our study. I gave her a ride. Everyone else is on their way," he explained. Wynn noticed that the young lady looked very disappointed that Alex had excused himself from her company.

"It's very rude to leave her standing alone to speak to

another woman, don't you think?" Wynn asked him. His face heated. The thought must not have occurred to him.

"You're right. Excuse me." He went back to the counter and apologized to the lady. Wynn licked her ice cream and watched the woman smile and shake her head, excusing the young doctor's lack of manners. She shivered. After she finished her ice cream, she would have to get a cup of hot cocoa to warm up.

A group of late twenty-somethings suddenly converged on Alex and his date. Laughter emanated from the crowd. By their sophisticated dark coats and well-managed, stylish haircuts, Wynn guessed them all to be young business professionals, definitely out of college and established in the 'real world.' A few years ago, she would have automatically labeled them snobs, but she was doing better about not judging people. She left off studying the good-looking group.

She continued to enjoy her treat, breaking off pieces of the sweet cone and using the broken bits as spoons for the ice cream.

"She's not alone anymore. Now may I speak to you?"

She looked up at Alex. He towered above her when she was sitting. He had a tall paper cup in one hand and a foot long sub sandwich in the other.

"You're eating ice cream?" he questioned the obvious when she did not immediately answer. She looked down at her mangled waffle cone.

"You don't like ice cream?"

He grinned. "Not when it's below forty degrees outside."

"Oh."

He stared at her, waiting.

"Oh! Yeah, yes, you may speak with me," she said, when she realized he was waiting for her permission to sit. He took the chair across from her.

"Mint chocolate chip?" he asked, gesturing to her half-eaten cone. She nodded.

"Good stuff," he said. He pointed to his chin. "You have a little right here."

She felt herself blushing as she reached for a napkin. The dispenser was jammed. Alex held out one of the napkins he'd been given with his meal.

"Thank you," she mumbled, swiping her chin. He began unwrapping his sandwich.

"Christmas shopping?" he questioned, gesturing to the bags spilling out from under the table.

"Um, yeah. Just finishing up," Wynn answered. Her look was incredulous. She wasn't sure what Alex wanted and he seemed in no hurry to divulge the information.

Lord, what's going on here? she silently wondered. She stared at Alex, waiting for him to say something. When he only closed his eyes for a silent prayer and then started on his supper, she searched for something to say.

"I'm glad you found a church," her eyes straying toward the Bible study group. Alex's striking blue eyes followed her gaze.

"Actually, I still haven't found a church home. My friends, Steve and Melissa, attend this group and I started going because of them. They're not here tonight because they just had a baby this week. A boy.

"We're all from several different churches. It's a great group." He paused.

"That's what I wanted to talk to you about, actually. I've wanted to attend Living Branch again, but I know that

that is where you worship. I was wondering if it would bother you if I visited again."

Wynn was surprised by his considerateness. She found herself curious about what kind of man he was. His asking showed respect, understanding, and compassion. It also showed that he was sincere in his relationship with Christ.

"I don't think it would bother me," she finally replied. "Gabe goes to Living Branch, as well. I don't think he would be affected by your presence, but you may want to ask him."

Alex nodded. "Thank you. How can I get a hold of him?"

Wynn considered giving him her brother's phone number.

"I'll have him call you. Is your number in the phone book?"

He nodded and took another bite. He looked so comfortable sitting there. Wynn wondered how he could be calmly chewing his fully loaded, steak and cheese sub while such a confused torrent of emotions swirled around inside of her. He had to be daft not to find the situation unusual and awkward. She found herself again wondering what he was really like. What had happened to him after the wreck? She had not really known him before the accident. He had been incredibly popular and she had been incredibly not. She remembered having a class with him once. He was smart.

"What do you want to know?" he suddenly asked, causing Wynn to wonder of she had said something aloud. He smiled.

"You're looking at me as if you were trying to figure me out."

"I am," she said candidly.

"What do you want to figure out? What do you want to know?"

Wynn shrugged. She wanted to know many things. "Why did you become a doctor?"

Alex inhaled deeply as if unready for the question. His smile faded and his eyes grew serious.

"Because of Hope."

51

"Hope? My Hope?" Wynn demanded. He nodded. "Why?"

"Are you sure you want to hear this?"

This time she nodded.

"When our cars impacted I hit my head and blacked out. When I came to, I climbed out of my truck and the car wasn't on the road anymore. I looked over the edge and could see it down the hill. I called 911 from my cell phone. Then I heard crying. I dropped the phone and slid down the hill. Hope was still alive."

Wynn gasped. She had not known this. She had not read the police reports or the newspaper accounts. She felt the tears rushing to her eyes, but she nodded, asking him to continue. He clenched his jaw and looked away. She could see the muscles in his neck tighten.

"She had stopped crying by then. She asked me if I were an angel. She asked me to hold her hand. I was holding her hand when she died."

The tears clung to her bottom lashes and then slipped down her cheeks, making tiny splashes on the tabletop. Her chest felt compressed, but not with anger or hurt. It was love for her family that constricted her heart and lungs.

"I'm sorry, Wynn." He apologized, looking stricken and helpless. She shook her head.

"No. No, I'm fine. It's just so much like Hope." Wynn dug in her purse for a Kleenex. When her search proved futile, she looked up to find Alex holding out another napkin to her.

"Thank you," she sniffled. They were silent for a few

long moments, Alex staring at his partially eaten sandwich, Wynn blotting at her tears, hoping her mascara hadn't run.

"You probably think I'm devoid of sorrow over what happened," he finally, slowly said. "I'll confess. I tried to forget it all and move on, but that didn't work out so well." He looked up. "I've always wondered what they were like. What they would be like now."

Wynn bit her lip. Part of her wanted to talk to this man, to confide in him. He had a part in what happened. They had both been forever changed by the same event. Each had endured the loss. Wynn suddenly felt a full measure of compassion for Alexander Chadwell. He had suffered the loss of her family without having ever known her family. He had been tortured by the memory of people he had never known, never loved. For a short moment, Wynn was willing to concede that his loss had been the greatest. She took a deep breath.

"Momma was always singing. She had a beautiful voice. She liked singing the oldies and hymns and praise songs. She married Daddy right out of high school. He was in his second year at seminary. She liked pickles and peanut butter—not mixed together.

"She used to make scrapbooks for each of us, and, when we were old enough, we got to help. She told us she loved us everyday and when we were in trouble, she gave us this look that hurt worse than Daddy's spankings ever did. I always thought she was beautiful." Wynn quieted. There was no pain in her words. In fact, she found that it felt wonderful to be talking about them again. She glanced at Alex. His look was intent.

"Chassity was twelve." Wynn laughed at the memory of her so grownup sister before continuing. "But she acted like she was fifty. She was the Redecke family pessimist. She took care of everyone, always reminding us to brush our teeth and dress warmly. Have you ever read *The Chronicles of Narnia*?" She chuckled as she waited for him to nod.

"Do you remember Puddleglum the Marshwiggle? He always reminded me of Chassity. She would have turned twenty this month," she finished in wonder. Twenty. What would she have been like now? Still as pessimistic? Still watching out for everyone else? Would she have learned not to take herself and life so seriously? The reflection threatened with a fresh bout of melancholy. Wynn shook her head, sniffed, and continued.

"Caleb was ten. He was the clown of the family. He could just enter the room and everyone would smile. He planned to grow up to be a preacher and a magician. The night before the accident, I was working on an art project for Mrs. Osman's class. Do you remember her? Anyway, it was a clay bust of George Washington and Caleb accidentally knocked it over. It was ruined." She began to giggle and had to take a moment to compose herself. "I ended up chasing him around the house, tripped, and bloodied my nose. He felt so badly for it. He was such a sweetheart."

Alex smiled a little. "And Hope?"

"I was nearly eleven when Hope was born. Momma always said I was Hope's mini-momma. I spoiled her. She loved bunnies and angels. She always wanted to sit in your lap or hold your hand. I remember one time just after I turned fourteen, I was crying. Probably over something stupid, I can't remember now. Hope crawled up beside me and laid her head on my shoulder. She patted me on the back and told me not to cry and that she loved me no matter what. That was Hope. We all adored her."

Looking away, she rubbed her nose on the tissue and dried her cheeks with her hands. What was left of her ice cream had melted and was oozing out the bottom of the cone. She wrapped it up with the napkin Alex had given her. Finally, she felt in control enough to look up. Alex was staring at the tiled tabletop, lost in memory. It was obvious his mind was somewhere else completely.

"Are you alright?" she questioned softly. His eyes seemed to focus. He looked up.

"I'm fine," was his automatic answer. He looked away. "They sound amazing. I can't imagine how hard this has been for you."

Wynn was amazed by the compassion she heard in his voice. How could she have spent so many years hating a man like this? She was finally beginning to see God's hand in the events of the past seven years. Why had she ever doubted Him?

"Alex?"

They both looked up to see the pretty girl he had come in with.

"Nichole. Wynn this is Nichole Garret. Nichole, this is Wynn Redecke," Alex introduced, mechanically standing in true gentlemanlike fashion. Nichole smiled and Wynn returned the greeting.

"It's nice to meet you." She turned to Alex.

"I'm sorry to interrupt. I just came over to tell you that Mike just called Steve and we're all headed over to their house to see the baby. Nathan and Mary offered to let me ride with them. So, I'll see you next week?"

"Uh, yeah. Tell them I said hello?"

"I will." She looked at Wynn. "You're welcome to come to our Bible study. We would be happy to have you."

Wynn found this very kind. "Thank you very much for the invitation," she glanced at Alex. "I'll definitely consider it. It was a pleasure to meet you. Alex and I were actually finished—"

"With our dinner and were going to do a little shopping," Alex finished quickly. He called out a goodbye to the departing group and said goodbye to Nichole.

"You lied to her," Wynn said with amused incredulity. Alex pointed an accusing finger in her direction.

"So did you. You had no plans to consider attending our Bible study."

Wynn raised her chin a little. "I intend to consider it and I intend to decide not to. You right out lied."

"Not completely. I still have to buy my mother a Christmas gift. Therefore I plan to do a little shopping," he challenged, sweeping her mess onto his plastic tray.

"But you clearly implied that we would be shopping together," she pointed out. A hint of remorse began to shade his features.

"I shouldn't have told her that, but I did it without thinking first. You were going to tell her that we were finished talking and I would have had a heck of a time trying to find an excuse not to go to my best friend's house."

"Why don't you want to go?" Wynn questioned nosily. Alex's look was sheepish.

"I didn't want to give Nichole a ride over. I think she was beginning to read too much into our friendship. I don't want to have to tell her I'm not interested."

"Oh. I'm sorry I asked. I didn't mean to pry."

"S'okay," he shrugged. He looked down once more at her packaged purchases. "Were you getting ready to leave when I came over?"

"Well," Wynn hesitated. "I was actually thinking of how I was going to get all this home. See, I share an apartment and today one of my roommates, well Ashleigh, from the ballpark? Her car wouldn't start and she had to be at work so I loaned her mine. I had to take the bus to get here." She pointed to the theatre marquee. "I was thinking of seeing a movie while I waited for Ashleigh to get off work and come pick me up, but that will be another three hours at least."

"I can give you a ride home," Alex offered, with a shrug. Wynn laughed aloud before she could help herself.

"What's funny," he asked, the corner of his mouth quirked, ready to smile.

"This is unreal. We can't be friends," she said more to herself than to her intruding companion. She was surprised by Alex's responding chuckle.

"I'm offering you a ride home with no strings attached. You don't have to ever speak to me again. Feel free to run away, screaming the next time you see me."

Wynn pictured herself bumping into him, white frocked and thoroughly doctor-ish, at the hospital. She could just see herself slap her hands to her cheeks, scream bloody-murder, and turn around and run away as fast as her little, white, nurse shoes would take her. Their juvenile patients would certainly get a kick out of that. Wynn shook her head and laughed.

"So how about it?"

She looked over all her packages. She really didn't want to wait for Ashleigh and she definitely didn't want to wrestle all her bags on and off the bus. But what would Gabe say if he found out she accepted a ride from Dr. Chadwell?

"You said you had to shop for your mother's Christmas gift?"

He nodded. "Yeah and I haven't the faintest idea what to get her. Last year I got her stationary that she's probably never used. I was thinking jewelry this year. Any suggestions?"

Wynn nodded. "A mother's ring."

A smile stretched across his face, carving out a slight dimple in his cheek. "That would work. I don't suppose you would want to help me pick one out, would you?"

"No strings, huh?"

"It was merely a suggestion," Alex replied in good humor. "But seeing as how a jewelry store just happens to be in the direct path we, should you accept my generous offer, will have to travel to reach my car, I might as well stop and peruse the selection. That will leave you standing alone in the middle of the overcrowded hall, holding your numerous bags, while I take an extremely long time using my thoroughly masculine brain to decide what my mother would like. Whereas, with a bit of assistance, the task could be completed much quicker."

Wynn studied the man for a moment, refusing to think about the easy camaraderie that was quickly being formed between them. If she weren't careful, she would easily forget who he was, what he had done. No matter how genuine he seemed, how friendly and sweet he appeared, or how startlingly good looking he was when he smiled, she could not, would not, befriend him.

"Alright, I accept your offer and will help you pick out her gift."

52

"This it is. Right here," Wynn announced. Her voice was tight. She cleared her throat. Alex turned the Jeep into the parking lot she designated. The apartment building was old and not in the better part of town. The parking lot was dimly lit by one flickering, humming flood light. Broken glass glittered on the fractured pavement.

Alex couldn't say what had possessed him to offer Wynn a ride. She obviously didn't want to know him, wanted nothing to do with him. But he wanted to know her. He admired her and her brother for living out their faith in forgiving him. He respected her for the strength she had developed through all the hard knocks life had given her. He felt camaraderie with her because of their professions. He genuinely just liked her. She was sweet, funny, and smart. He had noted the way she interacted with different people—her roommate, Clara, her co-workers, the sales attendant at the jewelry store. The kids at work often mentioned her name and his co-workers spoke well of her.

Alex shifted the car into park. Wynn turned to face him with a tension filled smile. The easiness she had displayed while they looked over the jewelry and even during the first part of the car ride to her apartment was quickly dissipating.

"Thank you very much for the ride. It was really nice of you and I really appreciate it."

"Let me help you carry your things up," he said, already with a hand on his door handle.

"No!" she all but shouted. "Uh, thank you, but I can get it. Really."

Alex nodded, not wanting to push her further. "I'll at least help you get it out of the back."

They simultaneously climbed out of the car and into the stingingly cold, night air. Alex sucked in a breath and blew it out through his teeth. A frosty white puff formed and faded. Wynn nervously glanced around the parking lot. Alex pulled open the glass hatch. The heavy metal door of the apartment building opened and Wynn nearly jumped out of her skin. She spun around so fast the toe of her boot caught in a crack in the concrete. She tipped sideways. Alex tried to catch her, but his hands were already full of bags. She stumbled, looking more than a bit tipsy. She landed hard against the Jeep. Alex fought hard not to laugh. Wynn's face was hidden, but she quickly righted herself and ran a hand over the metal of the vehicle. Her voice was full of humor.

"I think I dented your car."

Alex took her at her word and hurried over to inspect the damage.

"Only kidding," she reassured with a quirky grin. Alex smiled.

"How would I have explained that to the insurance company?"

Wynn shrugged. "Damage caused by gallantry? You rescued a poor student from the public transportation system only to have her maliciously charge into the side of your Jeep."

"Bet they've never had that claim before," he commented as he handed off the bags. "Are you alright, by the way?"

"You mean other than blushing with humiliation? Fine."

Alex chuckled and reached in for the last of her purchases. "I tried to catch you, but I was too slow. Well that's the last of it. Can I at least get the door for you?"

Wynn started to reply when a car bounced into the parking lot. The headlights suddenly flashed in their eyes. Alex held a hand up to shield his offended retinas.

"Oh, no," Wynn whispered. She hung her head in defeat as the driver of the blinding headlights parked and turned off the ignition.

"What's the matter?" Alex asked in concern, but Wynn didn't have time to reply.

"Alex Chadwell?"

He looked up to see Gabriel leaning on the top of his car door. So this was the cause of Wynn's stumbling jig into the side of his car. She hadn't wanted to be caught with him. Alex suddenly realized just how terrible his idea of driving her home had truly been.

"I can explain—" he started.

"Ashleigh has my car—" Wynn began at the same time. Gabriel held up both hands.

"I don't need an explanation," he said, with an evaluating glance at Alex. He motioned toward the building. "But I want one. Inside."

53

Wynn felt like a guilty teenager sitting before her father. She had known she should have refused Alex's offer. She should never have let him sit down at the table in the food court. What must her brother think of her?

Alex sat at one end of the red couch and she at the other. Gabriel was perched on a barstool. Ducky stood behind the island, not knowing whether to stay and watch the spectacle or disappear into her bedroom and listen at the door. Alex shifted uncomfortably.

"So?" Gabe, the judge and jury, prompted. Alex opened his mouth to plead their case. Wynn interrupted.

"I loaned Ashleigh my car and I took the bus to the mall. I happened to run into Alex. He offered me a ride home. I accepted because it would have been impossible to ride the bus home with all my packages," Wynn quickly explained, shrugging nonchalantly, as if everyone accepted rides from the man that had been involved in the accident that had killed over half her family. She swallowed hard. Gabriel's look was very nearly a glare. If he narrowed his eyes further they would close entirely. Wynn tried her best to look innocent. After all, what had she really done wrong? Alexander Chadwell owed her family. Playing chauffeur for an evening barely touched upon the debt he needed to repay. She raised her chin in defiance.

Her next plea would be insanity.

"He was only being a gentleman. Really, I don't see what the big deal is—"

Gabriel grunted. "I don't either. You're the one acting like this is an interrogation. Ducky and I were going to order a pizza. Do you two want one?"

Wynn's expression matched Alex's. They looked at one another in confusion.

"That's it?" Alex demanded in partial annoyance. "Aren't you going to yell at me?"

Wynn nodded. "Yeah! Aren't you going to tell me how stupid I was and that I should never speak to him again?"

Gabriel stared at them in amusement. "Hardly. Do you want a pizza or not? I'm starving. We had supper nearly three hours ago."

"I better go," Alex said, standing. His face was contorted with confusion. Wynn sat stunned by her brother's reaction. This was not at all what she had been expecting.

"Alex, have you read anything from the book of Joshua yet?" Gabriel suddenly asked. Alex turned.

"No. Not yet," he confessed. Gabriel nodded and circled the counter to the refrigerator. He pulled out a can of soda.

"Well, in Old Testament times, God commanded Israel to create cities of refuge, places where people who were unintentionally responsible for another's death could go and live. God commanded that they be accepted and given a place in the city. No one could avenge the blood of the dead by harming them. You entered that city when you accepted Christ." He shrugged. "We're accepting you and giving you a place."

"I don't understand how you can."

Gabriel looked to Wynn. She stared back, wondering at Gabe's capacity to forgive. How could he be so incredibly good? Why wasn't she more like him? Why couldn't she offer that unconditional forgiveness, the merciful acceptance? Then she looked to Alex. He looked so amazed and so grateful. Wynn was surprised to see tears forming in his eyes and her heart broke for him.

"We can because God did the same for us."

54

"I can't believe I let you talk me into this," Gabriel muttered, slapping a green and red, felt hat on his head. The silver jingle bell on the top rang happily.

"I think you look adorable," Ducky told him. She slipped a pointed shoe over her red stockings. He made a face at her and jabbed a finger in his sister's direction.

"You owe me big. My Christmas gift better be huge. A new computer or a motorcycle or something equally as expensive," he told her. She laughed. She and Ducky had combined resources and bought him a first edition Tolkien actually. It was the most extravagant gift she had ever purchased for him.

"I love you Gabe. You're the best brother in the whole wide world."

"Yeah, yeah, yeah."

Wynn tucked her hair up in the hairnet and pulled the powder white wig on. Her crimson velvet and snowy fur costume was very warm. She should have brought extra deodorant.

"If I overheat and faint, you have to drag me away from all the kids. Tell them I'm narcoleptic and had to take a nap," she informed Ducky.

"Only if I get to throw water in your face to wake you," Ducky said. She jumped up from the stool she was sitting on and struck a pose. "How do I look?"

"Like an imp," Gabe told her, tugging on her sleeve to make the sewn on bells ring.

"Cute," Wynn assured. She slid on her lens-less wire spectacles. "What about me?"

"You look like Mrs. Claus with Botox."

The door suddenly opened and Santa Claus appeared in the room.

"Santa, have you been dieting?" Ducky called out. Santa turned to the side, showing off his trim waistline.

"You noticed!" he said, a jokingly pleased smile on his face. "And my supremely athletically fit figure is causing quite a dilemma. I'm not fat enough."

"Use the old mainstay; pillows," Wynn suggested. He snapped his fingers.

"Good idea. I'll be back."

"He's a riot," Ducky commented, once he left the room. Wynn nodded. She had coincidently found herself in his company several times in the past three weeks. They were in the same Sunday school class, and while school was out for winter break she had been working some days, consequently bumping into him quite frequently. He was always friendly and polite. He made her smile. Wynn sighed. It really was a pity that Alex Chadwell was such fun to be around. She fluffed the fur at her wrist. He was a good sport, too. Their young adult group at church had put together teams of "Santa People" to go visit local hospitals, children's homes, and daycares. They were supposed to pass out gifts and share the story of the nativity. When Ferret, who was supposed to play Santa, couldn't do it, Alex, having just finished a twenty-one hour shift, had taken his place.

"Why does he get to be Santa and I get to look like I just walked out of a Keebler commercial?" Gabe whined as he shoved coloring books and other gifts into Santa's red bag.

"Because your girlfriend is an elf. Now suck it up man!" Wynn commanded.

"Better?" a very hefty Alex demanded as he reentered

the room. Gabe snorted.

"You look much fatter," Wynn agreed with a laugh. Alex looked offended.

"I'm not fat. I'm pleasantly plump."

"Ah."

"Here's your wig. The beard's attached. And your hat," Ducky said, tossing a bag of accessories across the room.

"Thanks.

"I think this is going to be the best Christmas I've ever had."

"Why's that? You enjoy dressing up as a fat, old guy who likes to wear red?" Gabe inquired, continuing to stuff the bag. Alex pulled the white, curly wig on.

"Well, there's that," he confessed, then shook his head.

"This is my first year celebrating the birth of my Savior. My parents have come up. And," he glanced at Gabe's pointed shoes, "I don't have to wear that costume."

Gabe gave him a deadly look. The door opened and a nurse poked her head in.

"Showtime folks," Patty announced. "Aww, yous look so cute."

Wynn and Ducky laughed. The men, however, did not.

The four of them each grabbed a sack of gifts and followed Patty to the recreation room. Children squealed when the quartet of North Pole dwellers entered. They spent the next hour passing out gifts. A chair was pulled up for Alex to sit in and take Christmas present requests. When the last child had made his appeal, Alex took out a children's book and read the story of the first Christmas. Wynn smiled as she watched this man, who only a few months ago had not believed in God, read about the birth of his Savior. She was struck by God's love of irony.

Wynn laughed when Gabe was tackled by kids. The children were all so sweet. The younger one's had every conviction that she was the one and only Mrs. Claus. When she finally waved goodbye to her adoring fans, it was only so she could visit the children that could not leave their rooms. She and Alex paired up and spent two hours making rounds through the hospital. Ducky and Gabe spent the time passing out candy canes to the doctors and nurses. When they met up again even Gabriel was smiling.

"Now was that so bad?" Ducky asked him.

"I plead the fifth," he said stubbornly. Wynn removed her wig and glasses. She fanned her face with a coloring book.

"I had fun."

"Me, too. I felt like a super star. There were kids wanting their pictures taken with me, I had to sign autographs, there were even a few nurses trying to lure me under the mistletoe. I like being Santa," Alex joked, removing his wig. Mrs. Claus threw her synthetic hair at him.

"Don't forget, Santa is a married man," Gabe pointed out, discarding his shoes with a vengeance. Alex pointed an accusing finger at Wynn.

"I witnessed Mrs. Claus flirting with a male nurse in the elevator."

Wynn looked shocked by the accusation.

"I was not flirting. I asked him if he was having a nice Christmas."

Alex smiled smugly and folded his arms. "You see? I rest my case."

"That wasn't flirting. That was being polite," Ducky piped up, defending her friend's honor.

"That was flirting."

"And I suppose you asking that aide for a glass of water was not flirting," Wynn challenged.

"No. That was me being dehydrated," Alex corrected.

"You were flirting with her," Ducky confirmed. Gabe shook his head.

"No, no. It was definitely dehydration."

"If he were merely thirsty, he would have made use of the water fountain. But he picked out the prettiest aide on the floor and asked oh so sweetly for a glass of water."

"I couldn't have used the water fountain because of my beard. Why do you care if I was flirting anyway?" Alex demanded, a vain smile on his smug face. Wynn made a face at him.

"I don't care. My accusation, which is true by the way, was in retaliation to your inaccurate allegation." She snatched up her change of clothes and stomped off toward the ladies' restroom. Ducky followed, jingling all the way.

"*That* was flirting," Ducky said once the door shut behind them.

"What?"

"He was flirting with you," Ducky repeated

"Oh stop."

"And *you* were flirting with him."

Wynn stopped short and spun to face her friend. "No I wasn't! Well, I didn't mean to. Did it sound like I was? I can't do that. Why did you let me do that?" she demanded. Ducky only laughed and walked on to the ladies' room.

55

Alex opened the door to his townhouse and was immediately greeted by the smell of smoke. Busby was jumping around like a maniac, barking and howling. His father was yelling something about the fire extinguisher. Alex rushed through the living room and into the kitchen. His mother stood in the middle of the floor wearing an apron over her Christmas dress. She had an oven mitt on one hand and one of his thick socks on the other.

"What is going on?" he demanded.

"I was trying to make a casserole and bake a cake. I thought I set the oven on three hundred but I set it on five hundred. And you only have one oven mitt so I used your sock and, and—"

Alex grabbed a dishtowel and used it as a mitt to pull out the charred cake and crispy casserole. His father dashed in wielding a fire extinguisher.

"Open the door, Joan. I'm choking to death," he hacked. Alex turned off the stove and fanned the smoking oven with the dishtowel.

"It was turning out so well. I wanted to surprise you. I've been practicing my cooking at home," his mother blubbered. "You had bought the ham and instant potatoes and croissants and pie and I just wanted to help a little."

"Stop crying Joan. It was an accident." Darren set the extinguisher to the side and heaved a sigh. A loud crash came suddenly from the living room. Alex dropped his towel and ran to the doorway. The Christmas tree lay on its side, the glass ornaments were shattered, and stagnant water seeped into the carpet. Busby sat beside the tree looking pleased with himself. Alex caught the swear word before it left his mouth.

His father had no such control. His anger filled the air with language.

"Fine Christmas this is turning out to be. Alex, put that mutt outside!" he commanded. Joan began bawling.

Just then the doorbell rang. Alex ran a hand through his hair and growled.

"God, help me," he muttered the prayer. He swung open the door, wondering who on earth would bother people on Christmas day. Clara Beetle and Oscar were standing on his front step. She was wearing reindeer antlers wound with blinking Christmas lights.

"Hello, Alexander. Is this a bad time?" she asked, peering around him to see his father wrestling with the downed Christmas tree, his mother wailing in the smoke-filled kitchen, and Busby trying to squirm past him to get at Oscar.

"I just got home from work actually. Busby decided to play lumberjack and, well—" he jerked his head in the direction of the kitchen. Clara had stopped by twice since Alex had begun attending Living Branch several Sundays before.

"I see. Well, I was just running over to bring you your gift." She pulled a tray of fudge from behind her back and pushed it into his hands. "I suppose I better be gettin' on back. I left the goose in the oven." She glanced once more toward his swearing father.

"I don't have any family around here so Gwyneth and Gabriel are coming over in a little while to share my Christmas dinner. Gwyneth couldn't go home and Gabriel didn't want to leave her alone for Christmas. Octavia's coming, too. Her family flew to England for the holiday. She stayed because she had a concert. Is that your mother?"

Alex turned to see his mother nearing the door, dabbing her eyes with the corner of her apron.

"How lovely to see you again, Mrs. Chadwell. Is this your husband? Hello, Mr. Chadwell. I'm Clara Beetle. Your son and I attend the same church."

Darren came forward, a scowl on his face. Alex edged away from the door, leaving the elder Chadwells with the task of entertaining the talkative Clara Beetle. His mother chattered away as if she hadn't nearly burned his house down a moment ago. He set the tray of sweets on the coffee table and set the tree upright. Some of the gift boxes were crushed and a picture frame had been knocked off the side table. He bent to clean up the mess. He had thought having his parents up would be an excellent time for him to tell his father about the change in his life. At the rate things were going, however, his father would be ready to pack up the Mercedes and head home before Christmas dinner was on the table.

"Well, Alex bought a ham and some other things. You see I'm not much of a cook," his mother was saying. "I'm an interior designer, you see, and I was just always too busy to learn how to cook. And now that it's just Darren and I there's really no point in my cooking for just the two of us."

Clara nodded in understanding. Her eyes suddenly brightened with an idea.

"After you've had your dinner, you should all come and have some cocoa and desert at my house. I live just a few streets over. I'd be tickled to have you all over," Clara invited.

"Oh, that'd be wonderful, don't you think, Darren?"

Joan asked. When he did not immediately reply, Alex looked up from the mess he was cleaning. His father was staring at the bundle of fur in Clara's arm.

"Is that a—" He leaned around his wife for a closer look.

"A skunk," Clara said matter-of-factly. She held Oscar up so that they could see his beady little eyes. Darren jumped back, a look of horror twisting his sharp features. Even Joan took a step away from the potential stink bomb.

"Don't worry. He can't stink up the place. He had surgery. You all just head down a little later. I'll expect you sometime after three. Bye-bye for now," Clara waved her farewells, raising Oscar's petite paw so that he might say goodbye, as well.

"Goodbye," Joan called after her. Once the door was shut, Alex returned to his task. His mother joined him, commenting on what a nice woman Miss Beetle was.

"Nice? She owns a skunk," his father pointed out, as if owning a skunk was something no nice person would do. "And she was wearing antlers. You're crazy if you think I'm going to her house for desert."

"You don't have to go, Darren. You can stay here and watch television or take a nap."

Alex fetched a towel from the bathroom to soak up the water that had leaked from the tree stand.

"I might just do that. I'm starved. When are we going to start on this microwave meal?"

Alex prayed for patience and self-control.

"Here," his mother said, tossing the towel at her husband. "You clean up the mess and Alex and I will fix dinner."

"Try not to burn the house down this time," Darren threw out. Alex wanted to punch him. It was no wonder his mother had never learned to cook. Why would she want to cook for this man? Poison him, maybe, but not waste her time cooking.

"He wasn't always like this," his mother said quietly when he joined her in the kitchen. "Even now, he can be sweet sometimes."

Alex shook his head.

"You have to overlook him. Forgive him. 'Love will cover a multitude of sins'," his mother quoted. Alex was learning the truth of that Scripture firsthand, but, despite all the love being lavished on him, he was finding it hard to offer it to his father.

"Sometimes love and forgiveness are hard to muster up," he muttered, fetching the spiral cut ham from the refrigerator. His mother smiled at him.

"But it's worth the mustering. God made it that way. He blesses us when we give it." She pulled the box of instant potatoes from the countertop and began skimming the directions on the back.

"This doesn't sound so hard." She glanced toward the living room and then to her son.

"Don't tell your father, but I bought myself a Christmas present this year."

"Yeah?" Alex shoved the ham into a roasting pan. His mother grinned broadly and held up a pot.

"Yup. Cooking lessons. I start next week."

56

"Gwyneth, honey, could you get the door?" Clara requested, as she pulled the pies from the warm oven. Wynn handed off the cloth she was using to wipe down the table.

"Are you expecting more company," she inquired curiously, as she smoothed her ankle-length, full skirt and headed toward the arched doorway. Clara shrugged and pulled an innocent look to the fore.

"Oh you never know who might just drop by," she answered. The doorbell rang again. Wynn pasted on a polite smile and pulled the door open.

"Alex!" she exclaimed, her eyes widening in surprise. Alex, however, did not look surprised to see her. His smile was warm

"Wynn, Merry Christmas," he greeted. She only stared at him for a long moment while his smile grew.

"Miss Clara invited us over for dessert."

"Invited you?" she repeated. She noticed then a woman standing just behind him. "I'm sorry. Come in." She stepped back, glancing toward the kitchen. She just caught Clara's little, round face peering around the corner before she pulled back.

"Wynn, this is my mother, Joan Chadwell. Mom, this is Wynn Redecke," Alex introduced as he helped his mother out of her wool coat. Joan Chadwell smiled broadly and reached for Wynn's hand.

"It's so nice to see you. What a beautiful woman you've grown into." Tears were forming behind the woman's smile. Wynn was a bit flabbergasted. She wasn't sure how to respond to this greeting. She felt a warm hand on her shoulder.

"Should we leave?" Alex asked in a low voice. Wynn mentally shook herself.

"No, no." She managed to smile at Alex's mother. "Mrs. Chadwell, it's nice to, um, officially meet you.

"Let me take your things. The others are just through there." She pointed toward the open archway.

"Are you sure this is okay, Wynn?" Alex asked again, once his mother moved on.

"Really, Alex. It's fine. Clara loves the company, and I thought we had established that we're okay," she reassured.

A corner of his mouth lifted in a quirky grin. "Yeah, I think we're okay."

Wynn narrowed her gaze. Just what did he mean by that comment and that crooked, almost mischevious, smile?

"Remember, Wynn. We can't be friends," he reminded, handing over the coats she reached for. She folded the garments over her arm and met his gaze.

"Too late."

57

Ron Redecke put the lid on the peanut butter jar and slid it back onto the nearly bare shelf. He carried the paper plate and unopened can of Pepsi to the small, laminated table. Lowering himself into the padded chair, he allowed his muscles to relax. He stretched out his legs and groaned.

"Mmm." He rubbed his knee and flexed his ankle. Shep lifted his head from his paws and stared at him.

"I'm gettin' old, Boy," he muttered to the dog. Shep whined. Ron broke off a hunk of his sandwich and threw it to the mutt. He bit off a large bite and washed it down with cola. The ticking clock and humming refrigerator filled the silence. Running a granite hand over his eyes, his mind filled with a growing list of things he wanted to accomplish the next day.

He was startled by the phone ringing. He plucked it from its base on the wall.

"Hello?"

"Merry Christmas, Daddy."

A smile inched across his face. "Hello, Sweetheart. How has your holiday gone?"

He leaned against the butcher-block counter.

"Wonderfully. I just got back from Miss Clara's house. She made goose and it was so good. How's yours? Did Grandma Red cook this year or was it Aunt Daisy's turn?"

Ron ran his fingernail along a crack in the wood. "I didn't get out to Grandma and Papaw's today. I had a lot to do. Thought I'd stick around home and take care of what needed takin' care of.

"I got your gift in the mail yesterday. Thank you. My

last pair were just about to give out."

"Are they the right kind? I looked all over and finally found them at a Tractor Supply," Wynn sounded concerned. Ron shook his head and smiled.

"They're perfect. My hands'll stay warm and dry.

"You'll get your gift in the next few days. Time slipped away from me and I just remembered to mail it day before yesterday. Sorry, Wynn," he told her, glancing at the calendar on the wall. A bright, autumn frocked farm hung above the month of October.

"It's okay, Daddy. Daddy?"

He could hear the hesitancy in her voice and recognized it. She wanted to ask him something, but was afraid of his response. He shuddered, hating hearing that tremor in her voice. He wished he had never done anything to warrant its use.

"Yeah, Wynn?"

"I know it's several months off, but, Daddy, can you try and come up for our graduations?"

Ron slumped against his prop. She should never have had to ask such a question. He covered his eyes again as moisture burned the backs of his eyelids.

"Of course, I'll come. I wouldn't miss it for the world. I need to get off here, Wynn. I'll call you later this week. Enjoy your break."

"Goodnight, Daddy." He could hear the tears in her voice and his heart hurt.

"Goodnight, Sweetheart. Sleep tight." He hung up before she could say more. He stared at the receiver through gathering tears. She sounded so like her mother. He threw the phone against the wall.

58

Wynn tucked the books she had brought in her canvas bag. Ashleigh had laughed at her when she had explained her plans for her day off. Stepping onto the long elevator, she hit the third floor button. She barely had time to hum through half a verse of *Amazing Grace* before the bell dinged and the door slid open. She was starting to step off when a man pushed into her, in a great hurry to enter the elevator.

"Sorry," he mumbled, but didn't bother to look up.

"Alex?" Wynn asked in surprise, stepping back to look at him. He raised his head. His eyes were wet. "What's wrong?"

"What are you doing here?" he quietly questioned. More people entered the elevator, pushing Wynn to the back. They pounded on buttons and the elevator began to move again. Wynn shrugged and settled in for the ride.

"I brought some Dr. Seuss books to read to Jaime Nichols. She's a Seuss connoisseur," she told Alex with a smile. He tried to smile back, but couldn't manage it.

"Are you alright?" she asked again as the car cleared. Alex started to step off and she followed.

"I lost a little boy today." The announcement was abrupt and harsh. Alex ran his hand through his hair and stared at the floor. Alex had started his five-month rotation on Inpatient Ward. Wynn knew he had been assigned to the Yellow ward team—chronic care.

"We've lost kids before, but not while I was standing right there. I couldn't do anything but watch." He looked up, his blue eyes dark with confusion and pain. "I can't do this, Wynn. Why doesn't God stop this from happening?"

Wynn felt helpless. What could she say? How could she answer when the question was one with which she had struggled so long? How ironic, how very like God, that He would ask *her* to comfort this man, that He would connect them in this way.

She reached out a hand and touched Alex's sleeve. Something her grandmother had said years ago came back to her.

"Maybe He just couldn't wait to hold him anymore."

59

"Thank you," Wynn said as she slipped into the coat Alex held for her.

"Welcome," he replied, bending to gather his Bible and notebook. He glanced sideways at Wynn. She looked nice this morning. She was wearing a white shirt and a dark denim skirt. Her hair was down, swirling around her face. Alex thought about paying her a compliment, but thought better of it.

Their friendship was steadily growing, but was still a bit tentative. They met often at church and work. Occasionally they would go out for a bite to eat after church. There had been a change since the afternoon he had encountered her at the hospital, the day he lost Kaden. There was an obvious connection between them, but Wynn was quick to draw away when she felt they were growing too close. Alex couldn't blame her. He understood completely.

He should just walk away, leave her alone, but the more he got to know her, the more he wanted to know. He sighed.

"What's wrong?" Wynn questioned, concern tingeing her features. Alex shook his head.

"Nothing. You haven't been to sleep yet, have you? Do you work tonight?"

"I slept for an hour and a half after I got home this morning. I'm going to go home, spend an hour studying, and fall into bed. Then Hi-Ho, Hi-Ho, It's off to work I go," she answered with a tired smile. She had to be exhausted. She worked nearly every weekend after a very full week of classes and clinicals. Alex knew how she felt. Medical school had prepared him well for residency. He yawned.

"You look worn out." She followed her comment with a hand-covered yawn. "You're spreading them."

"Mm, sorry."

"Well, I'll see you later. I better get home."

"Have a nice nap," Alex instructed. "Have a long nap. You're going to be worn out tomorrow." She smiled.

"My first class tomorrow is noon. I'll sleep a little before that. And when I get home after school tomorrow I plan to fall into bed and sleep until I have to get up for classes on Tuesday."

"Sounds like a good plan to me. See ya later, Wynn."

"Bye." She waved and turned to go. Suddenly she spun back around. "Oh! Alex?"

"Yeah?"

"Ducky has a concert on Thursday. I wondered if you would like to go with me. Gabe can't make it and Ashleigh has something going on. It's at seven."

"Seven?" He mentally went through his schedule. "I can do seven. Would you— would you like to have dinner after?"

Wynn hesitated. Finally she smiled. "Yes, I would. That would be nice."

"I'll pick you up at your place at six-thirty then?"

She nodded. "Alright. See ya Thursday."

"See ya." He watched her hurry away as a slow smile crept over his face.

"And just what was all that about?"

Alex spun around to see a smirking Clara Beetle.

"What are you—"

"You know perfectly well what I'm talking about. What are your intentions concerning, Gwyneth?"

He held up his hands. "Clara, she asked me to accompany

her to a concert. I—"

Clara pointed a finger at him. "You like her. Don't deny it."

Alex laughed aloud, shook his head, and tucked his Bible under his arm.

"What is so funny?" Clara demanded, her bony, arthritic hands going to her hips.

"You are. You know better than anyone how it is between Wynn and me."

Clara raised a brow. "What I know is that the past has been forgiven, you can move on now, and yet you still seek her out."

"I respect her and, I'll admit it, admire her," Alex responded with a shrug. He fished in his pocket for his key ring. This conversation was over. Unfortunately, Clara didn't think so. She put a hand on his arm.

"It worries me, Alex. You two are becoming very fond of one another. Anyone can see it. But what happened will always be there. You two need to talk before one or the other of you falls in love."

Alex laughed again at the absurdity of Clara Beetle's concern. "Miss Clara, I have no intention of falling in love with Wynn Redecke. And she, I can assure you, has no intention of falling in love with me. It's by God's grace that we're barely even friends.

"And I don't seek her out. We work at the same hospital. We attend the same church. We're bound to run into one another often."

Clara shook her head and turned away from him.

"Miss Clara," he called out, amusement still evident in his voice. She whirled around and stuck a knotted finger under his nose.

"I just hope you're talking to the Lord about this, Dr. Chadwell, because heaven help you if that little girl gets hurt again."

60

"I have such artsy roommates," Wynn commented with a sigh. She stabbed at her salad. Ducky had sung beautifully that evening. Normally Wynn was not jealous of her friends, but this night she had felt a sharp prick of envy.

"Do you wish you were an artist or concert soprano instead of a nurse?" Alex questioned curiously. Wynn studied the question.

"No. But sometimes my job just seems so insignificant next to theirs."

"Insignificant?" Alex laughed. "Wynn, you save children's lives. You call that insignificant?"

Wynn allowed a smile to peep through. "Well, when you put it that way. I think it's just that I am so close to graduating, to career permanency, that I'm having a few doubts about myself and what I have chosen to do."

"Well believe me when I say you are awesome at what you do. The kids tell me you're their favorite care assistant," he encouraged. She smiled again.

"Thank you, but I wasn't fishing for compliments."

Alex shrugged and replied lightly. "Sounded like it to me."

"Hey!" she objected with false indignation. He stroked his chin thoughtfully, intent on teasing her.

"You know, Ducky really does have a beautiful voice. And Ashleigh, wow! She's talented. They'll both be famous someday. And there you'll be: only making sick children well again. Just taking care of them and loving through the hardest times of their lives. How menial!"

"Point taken," Wynn surrendered. Alex turned serious.

"Your roommates are talented. God has really gifted them. But, Wynn, you have been just as blessed. What you do is wonderful. Who you are is wonderful."

Wynn lowered her eyes and felt her cheeks warming. Something akin to joy splashed over her as he spoke. She was amazed at how much Alex's praise meant to her.

"So," Alex started, changing the subject, "how's Gabe? I haven't seen much of him since Christmas."

Wynn looked up, her cheeks still a bit pink. "He's been so busy."

"Runs in the family," was his comment. She quirked one corner of her mouth.

"He's working on his senior project and has an internship. He's deciding on graduate schools, he's still an RA, and he's working some with a friend's dad, painting. I talked to him yesterday and he fell asleep on the phone.

"Did I mention that your mom called me?" She laughed at the look on Alex's face.

"My mother called you?" he asked in disbelief. She nodded and took a sip of her raspberry tea. A waiter interrupted the conversation and Alex assured him that everything was fine and then turned back to Wynn.

"What did she want?"

Wynn smoothed a wrinkle in the white tablecloth. "She told me that she was coming for a visit and asked if I could join the two of you for lunch sometime over the weekend."

Alex leaned back in the high-backed, mahogany chair. His look was one of interest.

"And your answer?"

"I told her I would check my schedule and let you know. I wanted to ask you if it was okay first," she told him honestly.

"I'd love to have you join us. Would Sunday work for you? After church?"

"Mhmm," she replied. He smiled, nodded, and started on his medium rare porterhouse steak. Wynn returned to her salad, wielding her fork much more gently. It suddenly didn't matter that Ducky could sing like an angel or that Ashleigh could draw beautifully. She was perfectly happy just as she was. And that was a wonderful feeling.

61

"Try throwing it over the plate this time!" the batter yelled at Alex. He scowled.

"Try swinging at it when I do!" he shouted back. The batter smirked, unaffected by his response. He ground the ball into his mitt and kicked at the dirt. He was not a spectacular pitcher and never had been. He was a second baseman and a hard hitter, but not a pitcher. His left-handed opponent should give him a little credit for doing as well as he was doing.

Alex wound up and let the ball fly. His body tensed waiting for the whack of the bat. The batter swung hard and the ball reversed at the force of the slugger. The ball sailed into left field, landing mere inches from the fence. It bounced along the ground, off the chain link, and finally came to rest in the new grass. Alex whistled through his teeth.

"Very nice."

"Why, thank you."

"You get to go get it," Alex announced, flexing his glove and adjusting his baseball cap.

"Oh, no, no, no, no, no. I was softball fetcher when you batted. It's your turn, Doctor Chadwell."

"Aw, come on. It's way out there," he reminded pointing with his glove to the expanse of outfield.

"I know. I'm a good hitter."

Alex grinned and began jogging toward leftfield. He scooped up the ball with his mitt and threw it in to home plate. Now that was an impressive pitch.

"Showoff," was Wynn's comment when he returned to

the infield. He shrugged. He wasn't going to deny it. She picked up the mud-stained leather and turned it round in her hand. She glanced into the fair, afternoon sky. The rain-heavy clouds of the morning had passed on through. The sky was left empty of everything but sunlight. When she looked back toward the greening earth, she had to blink several times to wash out the sunshine. She slid on the sunglasses that dangled from the round neckline of her t-shirt.

"I've always loved spring," Wynn said, tossing the ball into the air and catching it barehanded. She tossed it again and Alex snatched it from the air.

"I love all the seasons. Baseball season, football season, and basketball season."

Wynn rolled her eyes. "Men and their sports."

Alex reached out and smacked the brim of her navy baseball cap back, causing it to fly off her head and into the damp dirt.

"Hey!" She picked up the hat and slapped it against his arm to send the dust flying. He stood still for the beating. She pulled her burnished ponytail through the cap and returned it to her head.

"Do you have to get home or would you like me to buy you supper?" Alex asked her as they bent to gather up the sports equipment.

"I have lots of finals to study for. Ducky and I are going to help one another study tonight. Otherwise I would have loved to let you buy me supper," she replied with a smile. She handed him the wooden baseball bat. The black lettering had been worn away from much use and the knob at the end of the handle was starting to split. Another good hit and that bat would splinter.

"A compromise then. We'll run by the drive thru of your choice before I deliver you home to study," he suggested, dropping his glove in his bag. She nodded her agreement.

"You're a prince among men." She slung the strap of her duffle bag over her shoulder, but Alex snatched it away from her. He hung it over his shoulder and across his chest like a bandoleer.

"Thank you, sir.

"I promise, someday after finals are done with and graduation is over I'll cook supper and you can come over and have an eating contest with Gabe. I'll warn you now, though, you'll never win." She held her hand out to shake on it. Her hands were small, her fingers short and pudgy. She had little kid hands. Alex extended his own massive hand and sealed the pact.

"Deal. Speaking of graduation, my mom wants to come up to see you walk. She told me to ask if she could," he announced, glancing sideways to see her reaction. Joan had quickly fallen in love with the Redecke twins, especially Wynn. She had been amazed and touched by Wynn's sweet spirit and her acceptance and forgiveness of her son. Now Joan asked after her every time she spoke to Alex. Both her visits since Christmas had included lunch with Wynn.

"I would be honored if she came," Wynn answered, her bright eyes misty. Alex nodded.

"I'll let her know then. I've acquired the day off, so I'll be there, too."

"You did get the day off? Wow! I feel really special," she told him. Her smile was huge and brightened her entire face. Then the pleasure began to fade.

"My father's coming, too."

Alex was confused by her somber expression. "Isn't that a good thing?"

"It's a great thing. I just don't know how he'll react to you."

Alex felt a pang in his stomach. He and Wynn had become close in the months they had known one another. Close enough that the past had been all but forgotten. Wynn seldom mentioned her father, but it was obvious that news of their friendship would not be pleasant to him.

"Would you rather I didn't come?" he inquired, quietly. Wynn did not immediately answer. She bent to pick a daffodil that grew wild at the side of the walking trail.

"No, I want you to come," she told him. She fell silent for a moment.

"It's a strange situation, you know. I planned on hating you the rest of my life. Then God made me forgive you. And now look at us. This may sound banal, but it's a miracle. It really is. Only God could have planned our lives to interconnect this way. Trust me. If it had been entirely up to me, I would still hate you."

"Yeah right. I could have won you over," Alex teased. He knew she spoke the truth.

"Ha. You couldn't have made me like you. And I would have hated you more if you had tried." She again spoke gospel. He grew serious.

"I know. I praise God for what He's done. He's offered me forgiveness and acceptance from every venue." He was quiet for a moment. God had worked wonders in his life and he was grateful.

"Mom and I will sit somewhere away from your father. We'll congratulate you on Sunday, at church, and avoid you like the plague at the graduation ceremony."

"Which one?" she asked, climbing the hill toward the parking lot.

"One?"

"Plague? Which plague?"

"Uh, the Black Death," he said, his eyebrow quirked. She nodded and pulled open the glass hatch of his Jeep.

"Bubonic. Good choice. It's transmitted by fleas from diseased rats and causes fever, delirium, and swelling of the lymph nodes. Yup. Definitely want to avoid that one."

He shook his head. "You are weird."

She only laughed. She popped the top on her water bottle and took a long swig while he loaded the bags into the back.

"Let me have a drink."

She passed over her purple sports bottle and he downed the water.

"Thirsty?" she asked sarcastically when he handed back the empty bottle. She held it upside down and watched a single drop fall and darken the concrete.

"Just a little," he answered, wiping the moisture from his upper lip. "So what would you like for supper?"

Wynn pulled open the passenger side door and stomped the dirt off her running shoes before climbing in.

"I dunno. Anything's fine. Your car's a mess."

Alex glanced around his vehicle. Paper coffee cups were accumulating in the back floor and his dry cleaning was scattered over the back seat where he had thrown it when he picked it up the week before. Foil gum wrappers and pistachio shells littered the front floorboards.

"Naw. It still looks great."

"I thought doctors were supposed to be meticulous, very clean."

He shook his head. "A common misunderstanding."

Wynn fastened her seatbelt and rolled down her window.

"I'm going to clean out your car before your mother comes up. You can't let her ride around in this thing."

Alex grinned and put the Jeep into reverse. "She's usually the one to clean it."

"You're awful." She found an empty, plastic grocery bag and started stuffing paper cups into it. "You really need someone full time to keep you in order," she said, jokingly. Alex raised an eyebrow and glanced over at her.

"Are you offering?"

Alex saw by the blush in her cheeks that she had caught his meaning, but she replied lightly. "Too much work. I already have too much to do."

62

"My brain is going to explode. Boom!" Ducky threw her hands into the air for added emphasis. Wynn was upside down on the couch, her legs thrown across the back and her head dangling off the seat. All the blood was rushing to her head and the room was starting to spin.

"Mine, too," she agreed, righting herself. "I just hope it doesn't happen until after I get my degree. It would be such a shame to have spent four years just to have my head explode before I get to graduate."

"Very true," Ducky agreed, tossing her music theory text to the side. "I want a root beer float. Ashleigh has me addicted, you know."

"We don't have any root beer. I think there's some Bubble Cola or something like that in the fridge. It works just as well. Fix me one."

Ducky set about fetching the supplies. Ashleigh had bought Neapolitan ice cream so she had to dig around the chocolate and strawberry to get at the vanilla. Wynn flipped through her binder full of nearly illegible notes. The two had been studying now for the past five hours. Wynn's head was beginning to feel as if it was filled with lead. She closed her book and stared at the wall where an exaggerated portrait Ashleigh had drawn of the three roommates hung.

"When you get married and your last name changes, will you finally let people call you Octavia?" she asked suddenly. Ducky laughed at the unexpected query.

"Where did that question come from?" she demanded, letting a scoop of ice cream splash into a cup of cola. Wynn shrugged.

"I don't know. Guess I was just thinking about Ashleigh's wedding."

"My family calls me Tavy. I'd go by that. But my dear, old friends could still call me Ducky."

Wynn smiled. When she and Ducky were first acquainted she had laughed at the Brit's preferred name. It hardly fit her. She was very sophisticated, classy, and pretty. She looked much more an Octavia than a Ducky.

"Any way I won't be marrying anytime soon. I, unlike a few certain incredibly lucky girls I know, still have two years of school left. I do have the bloke all picked out, though," she said with a twinkle in her eye.

"Oh? Anyone I know?" Wynn questioned casually. Ducky shrugged and handed her a glass and a spoon.

"I think you've met him a few times."

"Does my brother know about this?"

"Oh, I think he has an inkling. So when are you going to find yourself a nice fellow, Wynn?" Ducky wrinkled her nose after a bite of her ice cream. "Eww. I got some chocolate in here."

"I'm going to wait and let the nice fellow find me," Wynn announced, sipping some of her float froth. Ducky settled into the green chair, tucking her long legs under her.

"You'll never realize he likes you. He could spout love sonnets and tattoo your face on his arm and you still wouldn't get it," Ducky laughed, daintily sipping creamy cola from her spoon.

"I wouldn't date someone who tattooed my face to his arm."

"That's not the point. My point is that unless he goes down on one knee and proclaims his undying love, you're not going to get the hint. Just look at all the poor blokes who have tried to get your attention."

Wynn laughed. "What poor blokes?"

"That Henry fellow that Gabriel plays basketball with. The missionary from Ghana that spent the summer here last year. Vicky's eldest son, the biologist one. Ferret, Danny the law student, Daniel the accountant. Grant from church is always attempting to make you smile at him. Not to mention Alex, whose favorite new pastime is flirting with you."

Wynn's mouth dropped open and she could feel an involuntary blush racing to her cheeks. She set her snack to the side.

"He does not flirt with me!" she proclaimed, immediately thinking of their car ride home. Ducky smirked.

"Oh no?"

"No," Wynn confirmed. Ducky continued to look smug but made no further comment. She returned to her counterfeit root beer float, while Wynn started scanning the flashcards she had created. After a few moments she looked up.

"He doesn't, Ducky!"

Ducky laughed and held up her hands in surrender. "Alright, alright. He doesn't."

Wynn nodded with finality. "Okay. Good."

She bit her lip. "What am I going to do, Ducky?"

"About him not flirting with you?"

Wynn set her glass on the purple coffee table and fell back into the couch cushions. "We should never have become friends. Why does he have to be so perfect?"

Ducky stared blankly for a long moment. "You mean, you really do—does he— Oh, Wynn, I'm sorry I teased you."

"It doesn't matter. Alex and I can never be anything more. I can't betray my father like that."

63

"The more I read the more I am amazed. This book has absolutely everything. I can read the same passage five different times and find something new every time," Alex said, patting the black leather cover of his Bible. Steve grinned.

"Pretty cool, huh?"

"Very cool.

"So what are we going to study next week?" Alex wondered, fanning through the Bible study guide they had just finished. The study had been on prayer, a subject that had helped Alex tremendously. The author of the guide had said that God had many names and to choose the one that felt most comfortable. For weeks now, Alex had been calling on God as his father. The personal, familial title helped him to speak to God more easily. God had become even more real and Alex felt much closer to Him.

"I made a list of all the studies that we can borrow from the church library. I thought you should choose the next one." Steve handed over a napkin covered with sprawled titles. Christian dating headed the list. Alex pointed to the letters.

"Is this a hint?"

"Well. Lissa suggested I include that one. She thought you might want to do that one on your own or that you and Wynn might want to study it together."

"Me and Wynn? You two have definitely got the wrong idea," Alex snorted.

"I don't know. Lissa's pretty convinced."

"She needs to become unconvinced. There is nothing

going on between Wynn and me. And there never can be because of what happened," Alex said.

"And if what happened hadn't happened?" Steve prompted, reaching for his glass of Mountain Dew. Alex shrugged.

"It did happen so why even think about it?"

"Because you have feelings for her," his friend pointed out. Alex settled back into the plastic lawn chair. He pushed his sunglasses up his nose and rested his head on the back of the chair.

"Are you ignoring me?"

He said nothing. He didn't want to discuss Wynn with Steve.

"Uncle Alex! Look what I made at school!" Abby had just exited the sliding door that led to the kitchen. Her tiny pink backpack bounced about on its straps as she pattered across the lawn. Melissa, carrying baby Stephen, followed her ecstatic daughter. She must have just returned from picking Abby up from preschool.

"What did you make, Squirt?"

"A flower!" She held up the tie-dyed coffee filter on a pipe cleaner. "I made it for Daddy, but you can look at it. Here Daddy."

Steve accepted the gift before pulling Abby onto his lap.

"Thank you, Pumpkin. It's almost as pretty as you are. Can I have a kiss?"

Abby puckered up.

"She couldn't wait to give it to you. I told her you were studying," Melissa said apologetically as she neared. She shifted the baby to her other arm.

"It's okay. We finished our study a little bit ago. There's my boy." Steve reached for his small son. He had a lapful of children and looked a bit like a youthful Santa Claus. Melissa stepped behind his chair and put her hands on his shoulders.

"So what did we interrupt?" she wondered before yawning. "Sorry," she apologized and yawned again.

"You should go take a nap while I'm off to keep an eye on the kids," Steve suggested, throwing his head back to look at the bottom of his wife's chin.

"I was going to go make you and Alex some sandwiches and I promised Abby we would bake cookies this afternoon," she said, rubbing a hand over her purple-rimmed eyes.

"I can make sandwiches and the cookies can wait 'till later."

"And I'm leaving anyway. I have to be at the hospital in a couple of hours and I have to go find Wynn a birthday gift before then," Alex announced. He gathered his Bible, notebook, and study guide. A huge smile floated to Melissa's tired face.

"Stop it. It's not what you think," he told her. Steve sent her a warning glance.

"I guess I will go take that nap. Thank you, Honey." She bent to kiss the top of her husband's head and then looked to Alex. "I'll see you later, Doctor boy." She hugged Abby and baby-talked to little Stephen before finally retreating across the yard and disappearing into the house.

"I guess I better get going. Let's do the life of Christ next," he said, waving the list of studies in the air.

"Sure I'll pick it up on Wednesday. Tell Uncle Alex bye, Abby."

"Bye Uncle Alex. I'll make you a flower next time," Abby solemnly promised. She squirmed out of her father's lap and ran over to hug Alex's leg.

"Deal. Bye, Squirt. Make your dad bring you to my house to see Busby. He misses you.

"Bye, Little Perch," he said wiggling the baby's fist. "See ya' Buddy. Thanks for making time for this today."

Steve stood and clapped Alex on the back. "Anytime." He looked as if he were going to say something more, but clamped his mouth shut. Alex narrowed his eyes.

"What?"

"I know you don't want to hear it, but I feel like I have to give you some advice, man-to-man. You and Wynn need to talk. Thing's between the two of you appear much different than what you say they are. I think both of you are confused."

"We're confused?"

"If you aren't then everyone else is, because the guys, the folks from the study group, and everyone else who knows you, would swear there's more than friendship between the two of you."

64

"What is this?" Wynn demanded, holding up a torn, filthy gym shoe. Alex snatched it away.

"That would be my lucky running shoe." He poked his head under the seat. "The other one should be in here somewhere. I've had them since my senior year of high school."

"I think it's time to retire them, Alex," Wynn suggested with a laugh and look of disgust.

"I can't retire them. They're my *lucky* shoes," Alex reiterated.

"Bronze them then. That would cover the horrid stench," she said, pinching her nose. Alex chuckled and tossed his fortuitous footgear at her. She squealed and dodged the smelly sneaker.

"Hungry? Here's a half-eaten bag of chips."

"No thank you. How long has it been since you cleaned out your car?" Wynn wondered, pulling change and M & M's from between the seat. Alex shrugged.

"A year, I guess. I'm a busy man."

Wynn shook her head in good humor and got back to work.

"I'm going to run in and grab a pop. Do you want something?" Alex questioned as he set aside his trash bag.

"Please," she said with a smile and a nod. He left her to her cleaning and headed inside. Busby tried to push his way out as he pushed his way in.

"Oh, no. I know what you want. She's too busy to play with you," he informed the lab. The dog barked in frustration. "I have to say you've got good taste in women, Dog."

There was a crayon drawing of a stick doctor with a dog on his refrigerator door. He adjusted the magnet that slipped so he could see the artist's signature. Dora Daugherty was back in the hospital. Alex flung open the door and pulled out two cans of cola. He avoided looking at the picture again—the reminder that doctors didn't always win and that God didn't take the suffering out of life.

"Your drink, my lady," Alex announced as he exited the townhouse and neared his Jeep. Wynn's feet stuck out of the back passenger's side door. He came close and peered over her. She twisted her neck so that she could see him a little. She grinned.

"Your car bit me. My sleeve is caught on something under your seat."

Alex laughed and set the cans on top of the car. Then he circled the vehicle and leaned in the door opposite her.

"Let me help." He reached under the seat feeling for the place where the sleeve of her blue sweatshirt was caught. Sure enough the material was snagged on a bare coil. She couldn't maneuver enough to free herself. He tugged and twisted her sleeve until the fabric came loose.

"Mm, thank you. My arm was starting to go to sleep," she told him as she removed herself from his floorboard. She shook her hand, letting the feeling return.

"Let's take a break," Alex suggested, pointing to the concrete stoop. Wynn gathered the drinks from the top of the car and preceded him to the step. She sat down and held a can out to him. He settled in beside her and popped the tab on his pop.

"Thanks for helping me," he said, motioning with his

drink to the dusty Jeep.

"It's been fun—and I've found three dollars in change," she replied, with a quirky grin. She looked so cute Alex wanted to kiss her.

He swallowed hard. Steve had been closer to the truth than Alex had been willing to admit. He set his drink to the side and lowered his head to his hands.

"Wynn, we have to talk."

She looked at him quizzically. "Okay. What's wrong?"

He searched for the words to say. What would she think if he told her he was attracted to her, wanted to date her. She'd laugh in his face—or never speak to him again.

"Father," he silently prayed, "give me words." He turned to face her.

"People are beginning to get the wrong idea about us," he started. Wynn's eyes grew rounder and her cheeks began to color. He sighed.

"Wynn, *I'm* starting to get the wrong idea about us. I've got it in my head that it could work out."

He heard Wynn's shocked intake of breath and saw the burning color drain from her cheeks. Neither of them said anything for a long moment. Finally, Alex shook his head and looked away.

"Tell me you haven't wondered if God could work things out between us and I'll never say another word about it."

Wynn's hesitancy confirmed the truth. He smiled despite himself. So she had.

"Daddy would never forgive me. I couldn't do that to him, Alex. It would be like killing them all over again," she whispered. "We can't ever be anything more than friends. No matter how much we think and wish it could work out."

They were the words he had expected but had wished desperately she wouldn't say.

"You once said we couldn't even be friends," he reminded softly. Wynn sniffled.

"And I was right. Look where being friends has led us."

Wynn needed him to accept this. She needed him to be sensible and nonchalant. For her he could try.

"What? To cleaning out smelly gym shoe-filled Jeeps."

She laughed and wiped her nose on her sleeve. "Exactly."

"Ah, but look at the rewards," he smiled, despite the throbbing hurt in his chest. "Three whole dollars in change."

65

The early morning sunlight sank into the dark paneled walls. The bed was covered with a wrinkle free, navy blanket. One caseless pillow sat on the left side. An opened duffle bag had been thrown on top the bed. The rest of the room was bare save for the wood-veneered dresser that was set against one wall. There were no pictures on the wall, no knickknacks on the dresser, nothing.

Ron pushed all the contents of his half empty closet to the side. He had given most of his suits to the Goodwill. He had kept only two, both of them Christmas gifts from his wife. He ran a hand along the sleeve of the navy coat. His rough skin caught on the fabric. Lilly had liked that suit the best. A blue and silver patterned tie hung around the neck of the hanger. He'd once had nearly forty ties. The kids always bought him one for every gift worthy occasion. Every day Lilly would pick out a tie from his extensive collection. She'd tie it, tuck it in his coat, and punctuate the ceremony with a kiss.

He rubbed his left shoulder with his right hand. He had not worn a suit since the funeral. Without allowing another thought, he jerked it from its hanger and threw it into his bag. He dug through his top drawer, searching for dark socks. His hand brushed against the Book he kept hidden underneath. He froze.

Slowly he pulled out the thin, leather Bible. He fingered the name engraved on the front. Tears sprang to his eyes. How could he still cry? When would the tears dry up? When would the hurt go away?

Before he could stop himself, Ron pulled open the front cover.

Happy Birthday, Daddy! We love you.

All their names were signed: Wynn's curly, round letters; Gabe's scratchy print; Chassity's uneven cursive; Caleb's fat, tall handwriting; Hope with a backwards *e*. Below their names, Lilly's neat, slanted script filled the space.

Happy Birthday, Sweetheart. I am so grateful God gave you to me. I am the most blessed woman in the world. I love you. Forever.

He snapped the Book closed. It held nothing for him—no comfort, no promises. God had taken everything from him and he wanted no part of Him any more.

Even as he moved to drop the Bible back into the drawer he felt the longing, a faint stirring in his heart for the God he had once known so well.

"No," he growled.

Wynn and Gabe had forgiven, had moved on. They were happy. But it was easier for them. They had been children. They had lost a mother, sisters, and brother. Ron had lost his wife, his children.

"It's not the same. Their hurt was different. They didn't love them like I did."

The anger and despair coiled within him, bringing comfort when nothing else could.

66

Wynn checked her hair in the mirror. She felt a small twinge in her heart. This was one of those occasions she wished her mother could have attended. She would have been here admiring her new dress, making her put on her cap and gown so she could take a million photographs. Chassity would have been a sophomore, just two years behind her and complaining about how those two years seemed like an eternity. Caleb would have graduated high school this year. That would have made three graduations in one month. Hope would have been a teenager, just leaving junior high.

Someone knocked on the bathroom door. "Wynn, if we don't leave soon you'll be late," Ashleigh's voice penetrated the wood. "Gabe and your dad are here."

Wynn swung open the door. Ashleigh's graduation had already taken place. Gabe's had been a few weeks ago. Their father had come up and stayed long enough for the ceremony and to celebrate his children's twenty-second birthday. Now he was back again, having arrived the night before. She had cried when she saw him. She couldn't help it. She was always an emotional wreck when a huge event took place.

Her father had stayed the night with Ashleigh's fiancé, Ben's family. In a 'small world' coincidence, he had attended the same seminary as Ben's father. Wynn was curious to know how the two men had gotten along during their visit.

"There she is," were her father's words when she entered the living room.

She smiled and spun, showing off the new dress she

had bought for the graduation ceremony. The thin, cream material was sprinkled with small roses. The flared skirt reached just below her knees, short enough to be covered by her heavy black robe.

"You look very nice and I'm very proud of you," Ron Redecke told her. He had exchanged his jeans and work shirt for one of his old suits. He looked as if he were ready to step behind the pulpit again. The sight of him made Wynn want to cry all over again. She smiled instead.

"You clean up right nicely, sister o' mine," Gabe complimented from the refrigerator.

"Not too shabby yourself, dear Brother," she returned, noting that his green shirt was wrinkle-free. "You ironed your shirt just for me? I'm flattered."

Gabriel grinned. "Not just the shirt. I ironed the pants, too. If that doesn't tell you how much I care, I don't know what would."

"Ah, yes. Nothing says love like pressed trousers," Ducky agreed with mock seriousness. She held out a small white box to her graduating friend. "Here, Love. This was just delivered."

Curious, Wynn accepted it. There was no tag so she pulled the red ribbon from the top and pushed off the lid. A wrist corsage lay nestled in green tissue paper. A card was stuck beside it. *For my favorite plague* was written in Alex's thin, doctoral scrawl. Wynn's smile was unstoppable. She lifted the pink roses to her nose and breathed in their antique scent.

"They're pretty. Who are they from?" Ashleigh wanted to know. Wynn looked up to see her father waiting for her reply. Her smile fled. She looked to Gabe.

"Alex sent it."

Ron's dark brows arched. "Alex?"

Ashleigh, Ben, and Ducky shrank back. Gabriel gave a warning shake of his head. Wynn forced a smile.

"Yes. Alex Chadwell."

Her father's face darkened. "Why is Alex Chadwell sending you flowers?"

Wynn licked her glossed lips.

"We go to the same church and we work together," she said. The tight lines around his mouth did not relax. "We're friends, Daddy."

He said nothing. He just turned away and gathered his suit coat from the back of the couch.

"We better get you to the school. You don't want to miss your graduation," he said quietly. He held the door for the ladies and the younger men to pass through. Wynn was last. She paused in the doorway.

"Daddy, it wasn't his fault. If you only knew him—"

Her father's eyes were wet. His face was haggard with the hurt of her betrayal. He shook his head and held up his hand.

"No more, Wynn." He moved past her, leaving her alone in the doorway.

67

Ron settled into the seat beside his mother. His parents had driven up today. Wynn didn't know they had come. It would be a nice surprise for her. He rubbed his shoulder, thinking of how Wynn had been so quiet on the drive over. He should have said something to her, but he didn't. He was angry and hurt. His daughter's smile had been soft and full of pleasure when she read that card. How could she have done this to him? How could she have fallen in love with the same boy that had taken away everything Ron had loved? The betrayal of it caused his eyes to blur. An intense pain surged through his heart.

"What are you doing to me God? Is this your final revenge?" he demanded silently. He felt the faint stirring again, the desire for peace. There was still a small part of him that wanted to run back to God and beg Him to take him back, but Ron had become efficient at squelching all emotion but anger and bitterness.

Ron flexed his fingers. His hand was tingling.

"Everything alright, Dad?" Gabe leaned over to ask. Concern creased his forehead.

"Fine," Ron responded through clenched teeth.

"Dad, Wynn has struggled. She's never wanted to hurt you," Gabriel told him. Ron didn't want another lecture from his twenty-two year old son. He'd had enough of that at Thanksgiving.

"Gabriel, don't. I've had enough of your preaching," he growled. His son shut his mouth and shrank back into his seat.

The pain was becoming more intense. Perspiration

beaded on his forehead.

"Oh, God," he whispered, as he realized what was happening. The burning seared his heart. He gasped for air. His entire body stiffened as the pain consumed him. Clouded and frantic, his mind flew over all his mistakes in a few agonizing seconds. In a flash of terror, he knew that it was too late.

68

Wynn's heart ached. The look on her father's face hurt her worse than angry words could have.

"Lord, what have I done? You said to forgive, to accept Alex. I've done that. But now I've hurt Daddy. The look on his face was awful. He looked as if I had taken away Momma and the others all over again. How do I fix this?" She sobbed into the toilet tissue. The ceremony would begin soon. She would have to walk across the stage and smile for all the people who had come for her. A fresh sob took her breath away. The tears cooled her flushed cheeks and soaked the neckline of her robe. She heard the heavy door of the lady's room open. Heels clicked on the tiled floor.

"Wynn? Wynn, it's DeJanna. Honey, they're starting to line us up," her classmate said from outside her stall door. Wynn wiped her face with both hands. She opened the door.

"Let me wash my face. Thanks for coming to get me. It'd be a shame to miss this, I guess," Wynn shrugged, pulling a half-hearted smile to the fore. DeJanna's eyes narrowed with concern.

"Is there something I can do for you, Wynn?" she offered.

"Thank you, but no."

DeJanna waited for Wynn to splash her face with cool water and rub the mascara circles from under her eyes. It was graduation day and Wynn would appear before thousands with no makeup and swollen eyes.

"Are ya alright?" DeJanna inquired before pushing open the bathroom door. Wynn straightened her stole.

"Let's do this." They left together and started down the hall toward the gathering mass of graduates.

"Wynn! Wynn!"

Wynn turned. Ashleigh and Ducky were trying to break through the security guards. Ashleigh was calling her name and frantically waving her arms above her head. A surge of alarm caused Wynn momentary paralysis. Ducky spoke to one of the guards and they were allowed to pass. The two rushed down the hallway, nearly tripping in their haste.

"Wynn." There were tears on Ashleigh's cheeks. Ducky's blush stood out like paint on her pasty face.

"Wynn, it's your dad. The ambulance just came. Ben's got the car. We're going to drive you over."

Wynn only stared at them. It was happening all over again. The tears were automatic. The moisture puddled in her eyes, but did not fall.

"Wynn, we have to go."

She allowed the two women to drag her through the building. Ben met them at the door and guided her to Ashleigh's Honda. They were nearly to the hospital by the time Wynn could speak.

"What happened? Is he going to be alright?" she asked in a whisper. Her face had grown pale and her entire body was beginning to shake. Ashleigh glanced at Ben and then at Ducky. Ducky answered.

"Alex says it was a heart attack. He was several rows away but he noticed him first. He and Gabriel gave CPR until the ambulance arrived. Clara drove Gabe behind the ambulance."

"He's going to be alright? He'll be fine, right?" Wynn demanded. "God let him live. Oh, God please don't take him."

69

Alex rushed through the hospital doors. Leaving his mother to ride the elevators, he had run up three flights of stairs from the parking garage and was out of breath. He searched the crowded waiting room. They were in the corner. Clara and Ducky were comforting Gabriel. Ashleigh and Ben hovered over the still robed Wynn. She was crumpled in a hard chair, staring blankly at the tiled floor. Silent tears ran down her cheeks.

"Father, please don't take him, too. Don't hurt her anymore," he prayed as he hurried across the floor. Ashleigh and Ben parted for him. His heart was hurting for his friend. He had done all he could for her father, but he was so afraid it had not been enough. Ron Redecke's heart had ceased beating. With the crowds and the confusion, no one could find the defibrillator. He and Gabriel had performed CPR for nearly five minutes before the paramedics had finally divided the crowds and taken over. They had collapsed in exhaustion and been ushered out of the way.

Alex dropped into the seat next to her.

"Wynn?"

She did not look up, so he tried again.

"Wynn? Talk to me, Wynn."

She shook her head and the tears began to fall in earnest. The emotional stitching that was holding her together ripped. She buried her face into his shoulder and wept.

"Father, help her. Heal her, Jesus," he whispered, closing his eyes to stop his own tears. He wrapped his arms around her and rested his chin on the top of her head. He did not understand why God was allowing this to happen to her again, but he did know that God was the only One who could get her through it. He prayed that she realized that as well.

He felt a touch on his shoulder blade. He looked up to see his mother, her lashes heavy with tears, standing over them. He nodded and she took the seat on the other side of Wynn. She patted her back and whispered a prayer over her. Wynn shook with her sobs. Ashleigh had to walk away. This was the second time she had to watch her friend weep for her family.

Gabriel was hunched over. His head hung over his knees; his hands buried in his hair. Ducky and Clara sat on either side, both crying and praying. Others who had come to watch Wynn graduate now gathered around her to pray. Pastor Leon arrived. Her grandparents were sitting near, tortured by their own grief. A few reporters showed up to cover the story of the man who had collapsed at UC's graduation ceremony. Nurses and strangers shooed them away.

70

"Is this the family of Ronald Redecke?"

An hour and a half later, Alex looked up to see an elderly doctor dressed in green scrubs with a bandanna over his hair and square bifocals. Wynn raised her head from his shoulder. Gabe stood up. Their grandparents stood and drew closer to their grandchildren.

"I'm his mother," Mrs. Redecke announced in a hoarse, tear-strained voice. "And these are his children." She put a comforting hand on Wynn's back. The doctor nodded. He spoke to Wynn and to Gabriel.

"Your father has suffered a myocardial infarction. A heart attack. His heart is extremely weak. Tissue death has occurred. The damage is extensive. We are doing all we can. I will be honest with you. At this point, the outlook is not favorable. We are running some tests to see if he is a candidate for a heart transplant. A transplant may be his only chance."

Wynn put her fist to her mouth to stop the tears. It took a moment for her to gain control.

"May we see him?" she asked. The doctor nodded toward a nurse.

"He's drifting in and out of consciousness. You may see him, but only for a moment."

Wynn reached for Gabriel's hand and together they stood and followed the doctor. Ron Redecke's parents and mother-in-law followed their grandchildren. Alex had to look away.

"Father, please don't let this be the last time she sees him," he prayed. His mother slipped her arm around him.

"Pray for them, Alex. God knows what will happen and He will hold them tight no matter what happens," she told him.

Clara wiped at her eyes with a handkerchief. "I pray they come through this with their faith intact. For Wynn to lose him now, after all these years of watching him run from God, cower from life. He'll carry his bitterness and anger to the grave and that will hurt her worse than anything else." She reached out to pat Alex on the knee.

"You know you did your best, don't you? You did all you could."

But had he? Had he not caused them to lose a mother and wife, sisters and daughters, a brother and a son? Had it not been for him they would still be alive. Ron Redecke would be healthy. The heaviness of anger and sorrow would not have weakened his heart.

Clara took his face in her twisted hands. "This is not your fault, just as the accident was not your fault. They all know that deep down. Gwyneth loves you. She'll remember that."

71

"Daddy?" Wynn whispered. Her grandparents stood outside the door, waiting for their chance to come in. The blinds had been pulled and only the fluorescent light over the head of the bed had been left on. She took a deep breath and looked at her father's still form lying in the bed. His face was ashen and dark hollows showed beneath his eyes. A nasal cannula had been inserted into his nose to supply him with oxygen. An I.V. dug into his skin. A heart monitor bleeped steadily beside his bed. Wynn had been exposed to these machines and their purposes for years now. They were lifesaving devices—necessary and helpful. Now the tubes and machines looked like intruders. Her father had no need of them. They were hurting him, causing him to be sick.

She reached out and touched the hard plastic of the bed's side rails. His hand lay on top of the covers. She lifted it in her own. This was the hand that had once held a Bible with great reverence. This was the hand that would tug his daughters' hair, throw the baseball to his sons, carry roses to his wife. He had misused this hand in the past seven years. The skin was tough and torn.

Wynn glanced back to her brother.

"Dad?" Gabe called, finally nearing the bedside. Ron's eyes moved beneath his lids.

"Daddy?" Wynn said again, louder this time. Slowly his eyelids folded back. He took a moment to focus. Finally, he rolled his head slightly so that he could see them. A shadow of a smile passed over his lips.

"I'm sorry I missed your graduation, sweetheart."

Wynn shook her head and squeezed his hand. He looked to Gabe who had silent tears on his cheeks. He spoke slowly. His voice was old, tired.

"You've been so strong, Gabe. Don't get weak on me now." He licked his lips and closed his eyes again. For a moment, he appeared to have lost consciousness, but then he spoke once more.

"I've let life beat me. I let myself believe that God had returned evil for my service."

He managed a weak, bitter laugh. "How many times did I see people return to Him on their deathbeds? How many times did I pray with them? Now look at me. Better late than never, I guess."

"Dad—" Gabriel objected.

"I'm not strong, Son. I've hurt for too long. I let the bitterness infect every part of me."

He fell silent for another long moment. Wynn was struggling to keep her tears back. Emotion was thick in her throat.

"I loved you all so much. I held your mother and sisters and brother and you two above God." He paused to rest. When he continued his voice was faded and slow. "Because of that I lost everything but you when they were taken. If God had been first, I could have borne it until I saw them again in Heaven. He could have—would have—sustained me."

"Daddy, you need to rest," Wynn told him, wiping the moisture from her face.

"Yeah, Dad. You need to get better as quick as you can."

Ron shook his head a little.

"I'm so tired."

"Daddy," she whimpered. She wasn't ready to let him go.

"God, please," she whispered, lifting her eyes to the ceiling.

"Wynn, don't blame God like I did. Don't give up what you have just gotten back." His brow furrowed in silent pain. In a moment, his face relaxed and Wynn sucked in a deep breath. Had he left them?

"Daddy?" she choked out. He stirred as if waking.

"I need to do something. Find Alex Chadwell. I want to see him. I need to talk to him. Go on now. Tell him I want to see him," Ron instructed, his voice growing thinner. Wynn wiped her nose. The tears were blinding her.

"God, don't let this be the end," she silently begged, but she knew her father was finished. He was choosing to end it now. She bent and kissed his cheek.

"I love you, Daddy."

"I love you, too."

72

The group had circled to pray just a moment ago, but now they were scattered around the room, silently petitioning Heaven. Alex sat with his forearms resting on his thighs. He had shed his blazer and loosened the buttons at his throat. His mother had brought him a cup of coffee, but it sat untouched on the table. Steam furled like incense above the dark liquid, rising like their prayers heavenward.

Alex ran a hand through his hair. He wasn't sure he was strong enough to handle this again. His faith was new and feeble. Already the guilt assailed him. Wynn would never forgive him a second time.

"Father, I feel so helpless. What do I do?"

Ducky stood then and rushed across the room. Alex looked up. Wynn and Gabe had returned. Surely, they bore good news. The sadness still coated Wynn's features, but the lost look had left her eyes. Tears were drying on her cheeks, but her face looked peaceful.

Alex stood, whispering, "Thank You, Father."

"He's going to be alright?" Ashleigh asked, an ember of hope drying her tears. Gabriel stiffened his jaw. The muscles in his neck tightened and his expression hardened in an effort to keep control. He stared unseeing at an abstract painting on the wall. Finally, he met the eyes of his friends.

"He's not going to fight it. His heart is weak and he's ready to go home."

A hush echoed through the room. No one knew what to say. Wynn raised her downcast eyes. The tears had caused the green to darken.

"He's saying goodbye. Alex, he wants to speak to you."

The air left Alex's lungs. How could he face this man? What apology could he offer?

"Will you see him?" she asked, quietly and without judgment. His mother put a hand on his back. She said nothing, but he felt her wordless support. Clara managed to muster an encouraging smile.

Finally, Alex nodded. Wynn stepped to the side, allowing him to pass her and follow Gabriel. The two men said nothing as they slowly trudged down the grey hallway. Gabriel was struggling to remain strong. Alex was struggling to accept that God was allowing this to happen. He was struggling for understanding.

They reached a closed door. Alex took a deep breath.

"Father, help me." It was the most common prayer uttered by man. It was a prayer God never failed to answer.

Gabriel pushed the door open and stepped to the side. Ron Redecke lay still on the bed. His breathing was raspy. The heart monitor kept a steady rhythm.

Several times Alex had watched death steal in and strip the body of life. Dealing with death was a part of his job, but now he could not look at the man in the bed. He was a man dying of a broken heart, ravaged by anger, weakened by years of hurt. And Alex felt responsible for this. He began to back toward the door.

"You came." Slowly Ron Redecke's eyes opened. "I wouldn't have recognized you. Where did they find you?"

His speech was labored, but clear. Alex halted in his retreat. He cleared his throat.

"I was in the waiting room."

"Waiting room? You were at Wynn's graduation."

Alex nodded.

"My kids told me you accepted Christ. That made me

mad, you know. That just like that, you could have salvation and still have everything else going for you." He paused and took a deep breath. "I worked so hard for Him for so many years and my everything was taken from me. I felt like my kids had betrayed me when they offered you their forgiveness."

He fell silent again.

"Sir, I—"

He raised his fingers to stop Alex's words.

"Let me get this out. I forgive you for whatever part you played in the accident. Whether they would have died had you not been there, I don't know. I'm sorry that I helped you to blame yourself."

His voice was growing thin. A warm tear splashed down Alex's face.

"Wynn has finally allowed God to heal her. Don't let her go back to the way she was before. Help her to forgive me for letting go so easily. I wasted so much time." His eyes slid shut as if they were too heavy. "You and all the good you do is the good that God worked from all of this. Forgive me for not seeing it, for not wanting it."

"You can fight this, sir. You can serve God again," Alex told the man. "A heart transplant! The doctors can give a heart transplant."

Ron's lips attempted a smile but couldn't manage one. His voice was barely a whisper.

"God's just given me one."

73

Despite protest and persuasion, Ron Redecke refused to be placed on the waiting list for a new heart. He remained in the hospital for five days. On the fifth night, Wynn went home to rest with plans to return early the next morning. Gabriel and Grandma Red were in the room when, just before midnight, he suffered another heart attack. He was gone.

Wynn wept. She had lost her father years before. He had not been the same since the accident, but that made the loss no less hurtful.

She twisted her hair into a knot and pinned it into place. The numbness filled her. She recognized it. Reality would come later, would overtake her. She would break eventually, but for now her eyes were dry and she could do what she needed to.

Wynn stared into the mirror. The make up covered the circles under her eyes and the redness around her nose. She ran a finger over her powder-hidden freckles. Her bottom lip quivered but she held back the tears.

"God, this is so hard, but it's different this time." She wrapped her arms around herself. "Father, hold me. I know you are still in control. I know that you'll work good from this. You'll redeem my loss. But I miss him. I miss my daddy."

Silent tears broke forth. She was sad. She was hurt, but the pain was bearable. There was no despair this time. She loved her father no less than she had her mother or brother or sisters, but she had been given the chance to say goodbye, to accept the end. And this time she was turning to God for comfort and not away from Him.

Wynn wiped the tears away, rubbed her nose with a tissue, and opened the door. Ducky was waiting in the room they were sharing. It was the same room she and Gabe had shared that first night after the accident.

"How are you, love?" Ducky asked quietly. Wynn managed a teary smile.

"I'm okay. It's still like a dream. It'll all hit me soon," she answered. Ashleigh came through the bedroom door just then. She had gone through this with Wynn before. She had loved Wynn's family, too. She had no words. Reaching for Wynn's hand, she gave it a squeeze.

"It's going to be different from last time, Ashleigh. I won't get all crazy on you this time," Wynn promised with a half smile.

Ashleigh bit her lip and tried to smile in return, but couldn't manage it.

"Wynn," she hesitated. She looked down the hallway toward the kitchen. "Alex is here. He wants to know if you can talk to him. If not, I'm supposed to go send him away."

Wynn took a deep breath. She hadn't seen Alex in days. Her father had asked to see him several times over his last few days, but Wynn had never been present during one of their visits. Alex had called and left messages on her answering machine, but returning calls had not been a high priority for her. She had wondered how he was, wondered if he would come.

"No, I want to talk to him. Could you give us a few minutes?"

Ducky nodded and Ashleigh stepped out of her way. Wynn was not sure what her reaction would be. She had once blamed Alex for what her father had become. Would all the old feelings, the anger and bitterness come back?

"Father, don't let it. I don't want to be like I was before. Let me grieve and move on. Hold tight to me, Lord," she whispered.

Grandma Red was in the hallway. "He's in the living room. Wynn?"

Her grandmother rubbed her nose with her tissue. "I'm real proud of ya', honey."

Wynn wrapped her arms around the old woman. Neither cried. They just held onto one another for a long moment. Finally, Grandma Red squeezed her tightly before pulling away. She let her pass without another word.

Alex was sitting on the edge of the couch, his forearms on his thighs, his head bowed. He was dressed for the funeral in a black suit. He looked up when she entered. They stared at one another for a long moment before he finally stood.

"Wynn." He said no more. He just waited.

"What did he say to you? Daddy. What did he say?"

He looked away. Wynn noticed the wetness in his eyes, the way the muscles in his throat tightened. He was trying not to cry.

"He forgave me."

He looked up. He opened his mouth to speak, then locked his jaw and blinked hard. Finally, he swallowed. His voice was hoarse.

"He apologized." The tears coursed down his cheeks then. He rubbed his large palm over his mouth. He wiped the tears away with his coat sleeve. "He apologized to me, Wynn. Why did he do that? How could he forgive me?"

Wynn was crying now, too. She knew now that this was what she had expected the first time. This was what she had thought would happen after the accident. She had expected her father to forgive Alex. She had expected the peace of God to fill the emptiness. She had wanted her family to have been this strong. But they hadn't been. They had rejected the comfort that God offered.

Now, here they stood again. She couldn't rely on her father's reaction this time. She couldn't let his actions guide hers.

Therefore I urge you to reaffirm your love to him.

She moved across the living room and threw her arms around him, burying her face into his jacket. They cried together, finally spilling the last of the grief and pain they had stored over the years. It was finally finished. Her father's forgiveness had finally released them all

74

They buried her father beside his wife. The sun shone brightly and the breeze was light.

The wind whipped her skirt about her legs. Gauzy clouds rushed across the sky, causing fleeting shadows to momentarily darken the ground. The air was warm. Wynn absently twirled the long stemmed roses in her fingers. She knew that her father was alive and well just beyond her reach. The journey had been difficult for him, but he had found the way again in the end. She could picture him kneeling before the throne of the One he had served once, run away from, and returned to. She could see him reunited with his wife and children. Wynn would be happy the day she saw them all again, but that was a long way off. She had much to do yet.

As the burial ceremony ended, she stepped forward to lay the roses at the base of the four stones.

"Tell them I love them Lord," she whispered. "And God, I love you, too. I trust you. Hold me close. I won't run away this time."

75

Ron had asked to see Alex several times in the last days. The elder man had given Alex a charge to look after his daughter and he had promised to do so. Now Alex could only stand by, able to do nothing to ease her pain.

The crowds of mourners had dispersed. Even Wynn's grandparents, aunts, and uncles had spoken soft words to her and left her alone.

Gabriel neared and put a hand on his shoulder. "We're going back to my grandparents' house. Take care of Wynn. She needs this time," he said quietly. There were tears in the man's eyes, but the peace of God was there as well.

Alex nodded, amazed and humbled by the love of Christ. Gabriel and Ducky started toward the remaining cars, but Alex put a hand on the man's shoulder. Gabriel turned back.

"I'm sorry." It was all he had to offer.

Gabriel was silent for a long moment.

"I know." They shared a brotherly hug. "Keep an eye on my sister."

He and Ducky left and Ashleigh and Ben followed them after a word to Wynn. Alex waited for them to make it to their vehicles before he stepped forward. He said nothing, just stared at the stones.

There had been much hurt, but Alex could now see God's love moving in spite of the suffering. They had, all of them, run from it. Alex had tried to bury the pain, hoping that in the forgetting it would disappear. Ron Redecke had attempted to hide from it, but it had worn on him, causing his life to decay and crumble. Wynn had clung to it, allowing it to fester and rage within her. Gabriel had faced it and offered it to God, and God had used him to challenge the others to do the same.

Wynn did not look up from where she knelt in front of the headstones. "It hurts, but not the same way." A thoughtful look furrowed the skin between her eyebrows. "I hurt, but with peace. Does that make sense?"

He nodded again. To anyone else her comment might have been strange, but Alex understood her meaning.

"Daddy lived more in his last five days than he had in the past seven years," she commented, tugging a tissue from the pocket of her black skirt. He said nothing and she continued.

"I used to think that because I was a Christian and because my Daddy was a preacher that we should be excused from trouble. I felt so betrayed by God when the accident happened."

She sniffled and wiped her eyes with her crumpled tissue.

"Now I see that suffering is a part of life. God doesn't cause the suffering, but He doesn't keep us from it. He brings us through it—if we let Him. I wish I had let Him sooner."

Alex knelt and rubbed his fingers over Hope's name chiseled into the stone.

"He tried to draw me to Him for years and I resisted. I didn't want anything to do with a God that would allow suffering. I figured I could make it better on my own, than with a God who would allow horrible things to happen."

"Do you remember the night you gave me a ride home from the mall? When Gabe mentioned the place in the Bible where God commanded Israel to create cities of refuge?"

Wynn questioned him. He looked to her to confirm the memory. She smiled slightly.

"I thought that night that we were doing something great and martyr-like, forgiving you, accepting you. I guess Chassity and I were more alike than I thought." She laughed and sniffled all at once. "I never thought about it until now, but those cities of refuge were representative of God's grace, of His love for us. *He* is our city of refuge. He forgives us and accepts us. He's always there, ready and willing to welcome us in, even when we've done wrong or run away from Him."

Alex thought about this, seeing the truth in the analogy.

"Your dad mentioned the good that God was working from all this. He used that verse from Romans: 'And we know that all things work together for good to those who love God, to those who are the called according to His purpose.' I'm still not sure I see the good that He's made of it, but I believe that He will work good of it. Even if I can't see it."

Wynn laid her hand over his on the stone. "I can see it. He brought you to himself. He created a doctor of you, when you would have been a football player. You have touched so many lives: all the kids at the hospital, so many from church, people at work, me."

She pulled his hand away from Hope's name and wrapped her cold fingers around his.

"Through all of this, God has given us an amazing testimony. Look at how much we can share with others. We can use what we've been through to help others. I don't think my faith would have ever been this strong had these things not happened."

She fell silent, a ponderous look on her face. Alex stood

then pulling her up with him.

"So what do we do now, Wynn?"

Much had happened in little over a week's time. Wynn's life was experiencing a drastic metamorphosis. She had finished college and had lost her father. Her best friend would marry in a month, leaving her to find a new roommate. She would have to study even more to pass boards and earn her license. Then she would be starting her career as a nurse. Things were going to be difficult for a little while.

"We keep going. You keep patching up hurt children and I'll keep caring for them. We'll keep praying and reminding one another of God's love," she said softly. The sunlight shimmered in her glassy eyes.

Alex looked upward. He could almost feel them all, Ron and Lily, Chassity, Caleb, and Hope, smiling down at them. From where they stood, God's plans and purposes in all of this were perfectly clear. Alex, however, did not have Heaven's advantage. He was not foolish enough to think this was the last difficult passage God would bring them through.

"And when the next hard time comes, we'll remember that God is our refuge. In Him we'll wait out the storms," he added. He looked once more at the polished granite that reflected their smoky images. Wynn followed his gaze.

"Together?" she asked, squeezing his hand. Alex couldn't help but smile a little. God truly had worked a miracle of their lives. He had weaved them together through loss and through faith. Their futures were intertwined and inseparable. He raised her hand and kissed the back.

"Together."

Acknowledgements

I must begin by praising God who works in spite of me. I thank Harold and Beverlee Chadwick who hired my father to replace their roof, were willing to read my manuscript, and thought it had potential enough to pass along. Thank you to Hollee Chadwick who believed in my writing and took such wonderful care of my story. I owe a great debt of gratitude to everyone at Bridge-Logos who gave my story life—I never imagined it would grow up into such a nice book. Thank you to my mother who let me stay up late as a child scribbling stories, and whose decision to home school allowed me to develop my love of storytelling. (What other high-schooler gets to write her history reports as historical novelettes?) Thank you to my sisters: Cyndel who first helped me create people who aren't real, and Bethany who always lets me read my stories out loud and provides me with synonyms when I'm not near a Thesaurus. Thank you to Kathy Williams, my creative writing professor, who taught me much about the mechanics of fiction, laughed at my pathetic attempts at writing poetry, and encouraged me to pursue my dream. Finally, thank *you* for reading my story. I hope you love my characters as much as I do.

More Exciting Fiction from Bridge-Logos

Alabastron
Judith Goulding
The two central characters in this well-crafted novel—Mary Magdalene and Simon the Zealot—are faced with a major decision: should they remain a part of their culture or should they follow Jesus?
978-0-88270-983-3
TPB / 352 pages / $16.99

David—the Warrior King
David J. Ferreira
This exciting fictional account of David's life focuses on the era when he was a warrior-king. Though this is a novel, it is firmly rooted in the Bible and historical accounts and brings David to life in a very compelling and realistic manner.
978-0-88270-929-1
TPB / 448 pages / $16.99

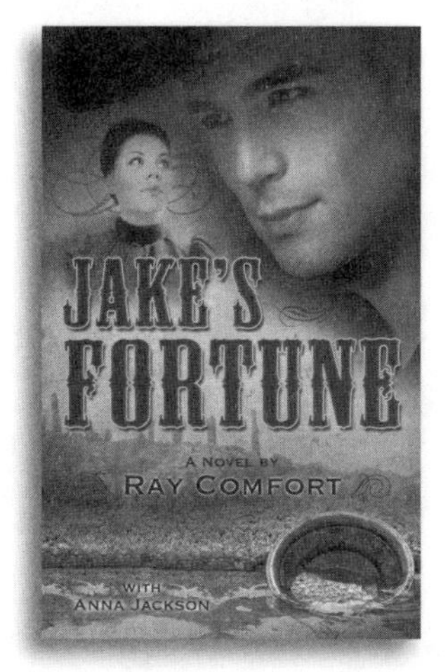

Jake's Fortune
by Ray Comfort with Anna Jackson
This is Ray Comfort's first novel, and his passion for the lost comes through very clearly. Men who enjoy westerns and women who like romances will find this well-crafted work to be very compelling.
978-0-88270-004-5
TPB / 344 pages / $14.99